CW00521965

PIERCE

The K9 Files, Book 2

Dale Mayer

Books in This Series:

PIERCE: THE K9 FILES, BOOK 2
Dale Mayer
Valley Publishing Ltd.

Copyright © 2019

All rights reserved. Except for use in any review, the reproduction or utilization of this work in whole or in part by any electronic, mechanical or other means, now known or hereafter invented, including xerography, photocopying and recording, or in any information storage or retrieval system, is forbidden without the written permission of the publisher.

This is a work of fiction. Names, characters, places, brands, media, and incidents are either the product of the author's imagination or are used fictitiously. Any resemblance to actual events, locales, or persons, living or dead, is entirely coincidental.

ISBN-13: 978-1-773361-45-1
Print Edition

About This Book

Just because helping out is the right thing to do doesn't make it easy ...

Pierce is on the hunt for Salem, a K9 military dog that belonged to Pete, a veteran, who can no longer look after himself or the dog. So the dog has been handed from owner to owner—until she's become too much to handle—and now the law is involved. No one has Salem's best interests in mind ... and they definitely don't have Pete's either. Pierce is about to change all that ... whether they like it or not.

Hedi, a young deputy, has lived in Arrowhead, Colorado, all her life and knows Pete and Salem but was helpless to do much when greed overtook his friends and family. She recognizes in Pierce the same qualities that Pete has, and, by Pierce's actions alone, she knows a corner has been turned. She also understands the locals won't take it lying down, and this means war ...

Pierce served his country overseas for many years, and seeing another veteran in trouble makes him realize the fight isn't over, even after life in the navy ends. In fact, this battle has just begun. But ... this one ... Pierce will finish. And he plans to win.

Sign up to be notified of all Dale's releases here!

http://dalemayer.com/category/blog/

CHAPTER 1

PIERCE CARLTON TOOK the next exit onto Highway 14, heading to Fort Collins. He wondered what he'd gotten himself into by agreeing to look for Salem, a black female German shepherd who might or might not be missing.

In theory, handlers and dogs weren't supposed to get too attached. Pierce had snorted the first time he'd heard that because how could one not?

Still, this dog was last seen in the community of Arrowhead outside of Fort Collins. Hence Pierce's stop here. If he remembered right, a small café was along this main boulevard that had absolutely the best apple pie you could buy. He pulled up to the café called Marge's. If ever a name could make you think of apple pie, it was a name like that. He went in and smiled. Right in front of him was a large glass case with lots of what looked to be homemade baked desserts.

His stomach growled.

A portly woman walked toward him. "Well, that's a sound I like to hear."

He looked at her in surprise. "Please don't tell me that you can hear my stomach from all the way over there," he joked.

She smiled and nodded. "My ears are trained for that. Come on in and take a seat. We'll get some food in that belly."

But he didn't want to leave the glass case in front of him. "What's the deal with all these treats?"

"Well, they're for sale," she said. "Is that what you mean?"

"Are they fresh-baked? Home-baked? Or brought in from a city somewhere?"

"I bake all my own pies here," she said proudly. "I'm Aunt Marge." She held out a big beefy arm and a rotund muscly hand.

He gave it a good shake and knew she did the baking herself from the strength of those arms alone. "So is there real food too, or do I just eat apple pie for the entire meal?"

"Nope, you're gonna sit down and have a good-size burger and some fries, and then we'll give you a piece of pie to top it off."

He hadn't been terribly hungry when he walked in, but just the sound of that made his mouth water. Obligingly he went to the table she pointed out and sat down. Within seconds he had a hot cup of coffee in front of him.

"What brings you into our town?" she asked.

"What makes you think I'm not a local?" he asked, looking around. "I heard you have the best pies around, but I haven't been here in many years."

"This is a small community. I know every person who lives here. The rest are mostly passing through."

"Well, if they know about all those baked goods under that glass," he said, "I wouldn't be at all surprised if everybody goes out of their way to come here."

She chuckled. "Enough that I make a fine living," she said with a smirk, and she disappeared into the kitchen in the back. He could hear her talking to somebody and wondered if this was a mom-and-pop place. She came back out soon with cutlery and a glass of water. "You never answered my question."

"I'm tracking down a dog," he said.

"Purebred? For breeding?"

Surprised by that line of questioning, he shook his head. "No, she's a War Dog, shipped home with her handler. He had to have multiple surgeries, then ended up in a rehabilitation center and wasn't able to leave. Since he couldn't live on his own, the dog got lost somewhere in all that."

"Pete Lowery," she said abruptly.

Startled, he looked up at her. "Sorry?"

"Are you looking for Pete Lowery's dog, Salem?"

Pierce frowned, pulled out his phone, checked the notes and said, "Yes, I am." He twisted to look at her. "Do you know where the dog is?"

"It attacked somebody," she said, staring at him hard.

He didn't know what she was looking for, but her gaze searched his as if to see which way he would go on the issue. His heart sank. "Seriously?"

She nodded, her face grave. "I'm not sure what happened, but she bit a man in the leg," she said. "She might still be at the police security yard, locked up. There was some talk about putting her down, but I haven't heard the outcome on that."

"Who could I talk to about it?"

"You'll have to speak to the sheriff," she said. "Give him about a half hour, and he'll probably pop in here for coffee and pie." And, with a smirk, she left again.

Pierce slowly stirred his black coffee to help it cool and wondered what would make a dog like that attack someone. Most likely a scenario where the dog was cornered and felt threatened or somebody she cared about was threatened. Pierce frowned, thinking about that until Aunt Marge returned with a heaping plateful of a burger and fries. Curious, he asked, "Do you know the story behind the dog attack?"

"Something to do with Pete's brother, I think," she said. "Ross said two guys were just talking to him, and apparently the shepherd took a dislike to one of them and attacked him."

"Dogs often see a threat we don't quite understand," Pierce said.

"I don't know all the details," she said with a shrug, walking to the counter, returning with mustard and ketchup.

He nodded his thanks, picked up a fry and crunched it. He loved crispy fries. And these were hot and tasty. He dumped ketchup on his plate and plowed through the fries. When he was almost done with them, he picked up the burger and slowly ate the beefy sandwich.

The meal was excellent. He'd come back just for the food. Aunt Marge returned once more, refilled his coffee and his water, but she didn't stop to talk this time. A couple other customers came and went, so the work was steady but not terribly busy. Pierce was about done with his burger, putting the last of it into his mouth, when a sheriff's car drove up. Pierce wondered at the timing. The sheriff was a bit early today apparently. Aunt Marge greeted him as he sat down and poured him a cup of coffee, then pointed at Pierce and said, "He needs to talk to you about Salem."

The sheriff snorted. "If there was ever a dog that deserved a bullet, it's her." He looked straight at Pierce and said, "If you come to collect her, you're too late. Somebody already stole her from the yard."

Aunt Marge gasped. "What? Now who'd do that?"

Pierce studied the sheriff's face. "Any idea who or when?"

"A couple months back," he said. "And, no, we have no clue who. Cut the fence and let her free. Hope they took her out back and put a bullet between her eyes. That's all she's good for."

Aunt Marge nodded in agreement. "So true. Last thing we need around here is dogs attacking innocent people."

Or rather people attacking dogs, Pierce thought to himself. But no use getting into that discussion here and now. Not until he knew the full story. But two things he did know: men attacked others without provocation, and dogs only attacked out of need.

Pierce highly doubted the dog would get an honest hearing with the sheriff though. That man had already made up his mind.

HEDI MILLER STEPPED into the diner, surprised at the odd silence around her. She caught Aunt Marge's gaze, whose face lit up with a beaming smile.

"There you are," she said, rushing toward her, arms open.

Her hug felt a little too effusive, her eagerness a little too grateful for her sudden arrival. Only it wasn't a sudden arrival. She'd been following the sheriff for the last ten minutes down the highway. But, when she pulled in just after him, she stopped to write down her notes. She was in a tough position. She was a deputy and loved her job, but the sheriff was getting harder to work with each and every day.

She walked to the counter and sat down on one of the stools.

"What can I get you, Hedi?" Marge asked, rushing behind the counter.

"How about a piece of that apple pie?" Hedi said with a grin. "If it wasn't for those fresh-baked pies, I don't know how often I'd make the trip."

"A lot of other good stuff is here too," the sheriff called out behind her. "And, if you weren't so uppity, you could sit at my table."

Her shoulders stiffened at his comment. Anybody else would have just let her sit wherever she wanted. But the sheriff was all about control, all about being the dominant alpha. Guess he hadn't read the most recent research that said there really was no alpha male in a pack. Still, the sheriff wouldn't share the leadership anyway. It was all about being the *one*.

She turned and glanced at him. "I was just going to have a piece of pie," she said quietly, "and then head on back to the Johanson place."

"What's going on there?" he asked. "Is there something you haven't told me?"

She shook her head. "No." She spoke in the same quiet tone. "No, I've told you lots. Same damn shit day after day."

"Well, you can't put too much worth into what that wife of his says."

"This time the kids were calling," she snapped, and she heard Aunt Marge's hard gasp. She turned to look at her. "Aunt Marge, you know what situation those kids are living in?"

Marge's eyes filled with tears, and she nodded.

"And you also know there's very little I can do about it,"

Hedi added softly.

Behind her the sheriff just snorted. "Nothing's wrong with Jed," he said. "He likes the bottle a bit too much. If he'd knock that off, it would all be fine."

"But the fact of the matter is, he doesn't knock it off," Hedi said. "And it's getting to the point that he'll do something serious that none of us can walk back from."

The sheriff waved his hand in a dismissive manner, as if to knock her nose back where it belonged. She just glared at him.

A sound on the other side of the café had her turning to see a stranger stand up. Aunt Marge rushed toward him. "Oh my, I forgot to give you the pie."

"No," he said, "you gave it to me. It's just my plate is so clean, you can't tell what I had." He picked it up and handed it to her.

Hedi watched, her gaze locked on the stranger. "Sorry, we're not usually so public with our dirty laundry."

He nodded his head but stayed quiet. He picked up his backpack, walked up to the till and dropped a twenty-dollar bill on the counter. Aunt Marge gave him change, but he just waved his hand and said, "Keep it. It was the best burger I've had in a long time." He turned to look at the apple pie in front of Hedi and smiled. "I have to admit it was pretty darn good apple pie too."

"Aunt Marge is a hell of a cook," Hedi said with a big smile. "She's got a big heart to match too."

He chuckled. "I can see that." He walked out the door, letting it slam behind him.

Behind her she heard the sheriff say, "Arrogant asshole."

"What did he do?" Hedi asked curiously.

"He was asking about the dog that escaped from the

fenced lot," the sheriff said.

She stilled, searching his face. "Why?"

"He's looking for it," Aunt Marge said hurriedly. "He didn't like that it had escaped."

"Was released, kidnapped, stolen," the sheriff snapped. "We didn't lose it, and it didn't escape. Somebody stole it, and good riddance."

Hedi glanced at Aunt Marge.

She just shrugged in a philosophical way. "I can't say I'm sorry she's gone. Obviously the dog was dangerous."

Hedi didn't say a word; she just inclined her head. She picked up a bite of apple pie and popped it in her mouth. Eating was a great excuse for not talking. She polished off her pie and then rose, throwing back the rest of her coffee. She walked to the register and left a five-dollar bill. "Thanks, Aunt Marge, as always." And, without saying another word to the sheriff, she headed for the door.

On the way out, she heard the sheriff sniff. "Damn women," he muttered.

Aunt Marge hushed him. "You know she can hear you."

"I don't give a damn if she does or not," he snapped. "We shouldn't have women deputies. You know that."

"Hey, times are changing," Aunt Marge said. "Girls have better opportunities now than just running little restaurants and baking pies."

"That's where they belong. You do what you do, and you're the best at it," he said in admiration. "And I do what I do because I'm the best at it."

"But that doesn't mean she can't be a good deputy," Aunt Marge argued. "You know she's always there for whoever needs her. She's the most conscientious of any of your deputies."

"Only because she's a woman," he said. "That's what makes her conscientious. It's a genetic thing. She should be staying home and raising babies. But she hasn't even got a damn boyfriend anymore."

Hedi stood on the front step and heard the sheriff push his chair back. She moved toward her car so he wouldn't know she had been listening. On the way she saw the stranger sitting in a big truck, the cab door open.

She walked to him. "What's this about you looking for Salem?"

At the sound of her voice he turned to study her. His eyes were a deep dark chocolate color with thick eyelashes. His face was lean and tanned, as if he worked outside.

"Is there a reason why you're looking for her?" she asked again.

"Are you asking professionally?"

"Deputy Hedi Miller, and…" She frowned at that answer. "Should I be?"

He gave a negligent shrug. "A friend is worried about the dog. I was asked to come and track it down. She was a War Dog and deserves a hell of a lot better than being locked up in a fenced yard for somebody to steal."

Inside, she felt her heart beat a bit harder. "So are you here for the dog or against the dog?"

He pushed the door open wider and twisted in his seat so he could look at her. "I'm here to save the dog."

Perfect. She gave him a smile. "In that case maybe we should talk."

He glanced back at the restaurant. "Not now. We got company."

She didn't turn around but knew it was the sheriff. "Exactly. If you give me your number, I can give you a shout later, give you the details from the case."

"We're not handing out no information no how," the sheriff said.

Hedi just smiled. "It's public knowledge. We picked up the dog. He could ask anybody, but he might as well get the truth from us."

"Don't you have something to do? Go chasing after those kids who are always whining." He got into his vehicle, turned on the engine and reversed out of the parking lot, taking off down the highway, back to his office. His tires spit out rocks behind him.

She turned toward the man, still sitting in the truck. "He's not quite as bad as he looks."

"I've met lots like him," the man said, his voice hard. "And they're a hell of a lot worse than they look."

CHAPTER 2

HEDI WINCED AT that because really the sheriff *was* worse than that. She was just trying to make light of his behavior. "Look. I don't know what happened to the dog, but she went missing about two and a half months ago. I came in one morning, and the wire had been cut. The dog was long gone."

"So somebody helped her get out of there, huh?"

She nodded but kept her face neutral. "It appears that way."

"I understand Salem bit someone."

She shoved her hands in her pockets and rocked on her heels. "Yes, she did. And, if there was a man who deserved it more, I haven't seen him."

A funny light filled the stranger's gaze. "That's what I would have expected," he said. "It's not the dog's fault then, is it?"

"In this case, I don't think it was the dog's fault," she admitted. "But you won't get anybody else to agree."

"What about Ross, Pete's brother?"

"You're free to go talk to him," she said. "It doesn't mean he'll be sober enough to give you any lucid answers though."

"How about you give me a map of how to get there."

She walked to her cruiser, pulled out a notepad she always kept close by, and he hopped out of his truck. When the door slammed, she turned to look at him. "We're here," she explained as she drew the directions. "You go up to the second set of lights down that road, take a left, another left and a right. "There's a ten-acre piece of property, no dogs, at least not now, and you'll find them there."

"Both of them?"

She shook her head. "I didn't mean Pete. I meant his brother, Ross. From what I heard, Pete is not likely coming home." She stopped writing and looked at him. "I could use some ID."

He raised an eyebrow, reached into his back pocket and pulled out his wallet, showing her his driver's license.

"*Pierce Carlton.*" She nodded. "Welcome to the county, Pierce. Just remember. The sheriff doesn't like dogs. Most people around here don't like dogs that attack."

"Nobody does." His voice was calm, neutral. "But I train dogs to attack. When it's the right time, they often save your life."

"You're a dog trainer?" She frowned. "You don't look like it."

"I'm a navy veteran," he said quietly. "Trained dogs for years. Been at loose ends lately. Somebody asked me to stop by and check on Salem and make sure she was okay and in a good home."

"She was but not for very long," Hedi said simply. She reached out and shook his hand. "I'm Hedi. Here's my card. If you run into any trouble, give me a shout. Better you call me than the sheriff. He'd just as soon lock you up as not. If you're not from around here, and you're causing trouble, he'll call you a vagabond and toss you in jail for the night."

"Nice county you got here."

As she walked back to the driver's side of her vehicle, she flashed a grin his way. "It used to be. Hasn't been for a few years now."

"When did it used to be?" He studied her with an intense gaze.

"When my dad was the sheriff," she said with a wistful smile. She got back into her cruiser, turned on the engine and headed down the road. She had more than enough trouble up ahead of her to stay here and brew some more.

If Jed had found that damn bottle again, those kids would be in more danger. The last thing she wanted to do was shoot their father in front of them, but she wouldn't let him hurt those kids anymore, not while she was there and able to stop it.

In her rearview mirror she could see the dust as the black truck turned off the highway and followed her. She realized he would be behind her for at least ten or fifteen minutes because the two properties, although not side by side, were well within walking distance of each other. When she got to his destination, she honked her horn, and, with her arm out the window, pointed where he needed to go, and then she sped on past. Gratified, she watched as he slowed and turned into the driveway. She hoped, really hoped Ross would be sober and could talk today.

Somehow she doubted it. Ross was nothing if not consistent. And this whole area had a problem with alcoholics. A lot of jobs used to be in town, mostly attributed to the mill until it closed. Then things got pretty ugly a few years back, savings ran out, odd jobs were taken up. Now most people lived hand-to-mouth, and it made them an ugly bunch.

What she never understood was how they still found money for booze. And it wasn't just Jed and Ross. Two other men, twin brothers, Billy and Bobby, were not only drunks but she suspected they were making moonshine in the back of their property. She wouldn't put it past them. It was the cheapest way to get alcohol, and they didn't seem to care if they drank one hundred proof either. Their guts would rot from the inside out, but again she didn't think they gave a damn.

She drove up to the front step of Jed Johanson's place and parked. Even as she opened the door to her cruiser, she could hear kids crying inside. She hopped out, walked up the steps of the house, rapped hard and then shoved the door open. It looked like she was just in time.

With a sigh she opened her arms, and two of the little kids raced toward her. All in a day's work in this job, damn it.

PIERCE PARKED BESIDE a battered old truck. What he saw was a run-down farm with an oversize barn and an open workshop/machine shop with several other unidentified outbuildings dotting the same area. An old tractor was parked outside on the left, and an even older car was parked on the right.

With his gaze sweeping the area, not hearing the sound of a dog or seeing signs of any other animal, Pierce slowly strode up to the front door, where he stopped and listened. There was no sound of anything anywhere. He reached up and rapped a knuckle. A startled sound came from inside, as if a chair had slammed down onto all fours. He waited a few seconds until the door was opened abruptly. He studied the swollen red nose and red eyes. "Ross, by any chance?"

"Who's asking?" the man asked belligerently.

"A friend of Salem's," he said calmly.

The man just blinked at him and then blinked again. "Who?"

"The dog you got rid of," he said.

"That bitch," he snarled. "Damn near bit me several times. And she did bite someone else. The brother of a friend of mine."

Pierce couldn't help but cheer the dog on. "Well, were you going to kick it or hit it with something?" Pierce asked. "They do tend to attack when provoked."

"I didn't do nothing to her," he growled. "She always had a chip on her shoulder."

"She loved Pete very much," Pierce said, keeping his voice even. "Obviously it was hard for her when he went into the center."

"Maybe. Doesn't mean she had to take it out on me." He glared. "The dog is not here, so what the hell do you want with me?"

"I was wondering if you knew what happened to her," Pierce asked.

Ross shook his head, spittle flying from the corner of his mouth as he did so. "Nope. After she bit Chester, the cops came, took the dog away and kept her in the fenced lot. Last I heard, some crazy cut the fence and let the dog out. I hope the dog bit him in the ass for that."

"Interesting," Pierce said. "And you have no idea who would have loved the dog enough to have saved it?"

"There was nothing lovable about that dog," he snarled. "She ate me out of house and home. Didn't do nothing. We had an intruder in here, stole all kinds of dog shit, and she didn't do nothing."

"Sorry, what was that?" Pierce asked in confusion. "You're saying somebody came in here and stole the dog's stuff? Like what stuff?"

"Dog bed, leashes, harness, blankets, that kind of stuff."

"Are you sure Pete didn't send somebody to collect the dog stuff, hoping maybe he could find somebody to take the dog?"

"Don't know nothing about that." He tried to lean against the doorjamb, only missed and fell against the wall. He quickly straightened himself so he leaned properly. "And Pete didn't say nothing to me about it." He looked around the room with a frown on his face. "All I know is it was stolen."

After saying that, Ross gave Pierce a sideways glance, confirming something Pierce had already suspected. "So what were you doing with the dog that she wasn't here that day the intruder came?"

He shrugged. "Don't know what you're talking about."

"No, of course you don't," he said. "What's the chance you were out hunting and decided, when the dog was taken by the sheriff, to just ditch the rest of the dog stuff? Not like you were taking Salem back in again, were you?"

Ross straightened. "No way I would. But I got a gun. I can shoot my own damn deer. She was useless."

"Maybe, but a dog can certainly flush them out of cover so you can shoot them, can't they?"

At that, Ross had the grace to look ashamed. He looked around and said, "A man's got to eat. Times are tough around here."

"Well, you'll starve now without the dog, won't you?"

"I got a job coming up," he said. "I'll be just fine."

"Too bad the dog isn't though." Pierce stepped back,

turned to look around and said, "Is any of the dog's stuff still here?"

He shook his head. "No. Whoever it was took everything. Every last bit of it."

"Okay. Thanks for your help." Pierce walked back to his truck.

The guy stepped onto the front step and called out, "Hey, what do you want the dog for anyways?"

"She's a very expensive, well-trained dog," Pierce said. "I would have bought her off of ya, giving you some good money for her. But, of course, since you let the cops take her away, and then somebody stole her, I guess I can't do that, can I?" He started up the engine and reversed out of the guy's yard, leaving him standing there openmouthed, as if he'd just lost a gold mine.

If it had come to that, Pierce would have paid to have the dog returned to a life she was better suited to. This place would have just been terrible for her. War Dogs weren't allowed to hunt animals, unless they were the two-legged variety. At least not the dogs he trained. It wasn't fair to the deer, and it sure as hell wasn't fair to the dog.

Back out on the highway, Pierce took the same road where the deputy had gone. He wasn't sure exactly what was going on, but he'd heard enough to realize it was ugly. But the useless sheriff, of course, wouldn't help.

Seeing her car parked up at the neighbors, he pulled in behind it and hopped out. So much caterwauling was going on in the house that he didn't think anybody would have heard his arrival.

As he stepped up to the front doorstep and knocked, he was correct. Kids were screaming, and Deputy Hedi stood nose to nose with a man holding a rifle in his hand.

She yelled at him, "Jed, put that gun down!"

"You ain't taking my goddamn kids," he roared, waving the gun around.

He wasn't pointing it at her, which was a good thing. Pierce looked around to see four little kids of various sizes—one in diapers and barely standing on his own two feet; two little girls who looked to be twins with tears in their eyes, hanging on to Hedi's pant legs. The other little girl, slightly older than the rest, stood off to the side, watching.

But it wasn't shock on the eldest kid's face. Pierce knew what was coming. He'd seen it before. He just didn't know how to stop it.

Just then Jed shoved the deputy back. "Hedi, I told you to get the hell out of here. My kids are just fine." This time he did raise the weapon, and he pointed at her. Even worse, he poked her in her chest with it. "Now you just get the hell off my property."

She was spitting mad, Pierce could see that, but she also didn't want to pull her gun and get into a gunfight that no one would win.

Pierce, on the other hand, didn't have any such qualms. He took two steps inside. Just as the man realized somebody else was in the game, he turned to face the new threat. ... Pierce had already pulled the rifle free of Jed's hands and slapped the butt hard across Jed's face, knocking him to the ground.

As the man struggled to turn around to see what the hell happened, Pierce pointed the rifle down at him and said, "Go ahead and move."

The ice in Pierce's voice had Jed falling back, so he was lying flat on the floor, staring up at him.

Hedi walked over and said, "Give me the gun please."

Her voice was calm but hard.

Pierce assessed her, then nodded and handed over the rifle, speaking to her but for Jed's benefit as well. "Nobody ever points a gun at a woman or uses it to push a woman backward or threatens her with it in my presence. Especially a woman in uniform, disrespecting both the woman and the office she holds." His tone was equally hard, even as he lowered his voice. "Never, ever in my presence."

She studied him for a long moment, then nodded. She opened the rifle, pulled out the two cartridges, disarming it, and placed it on the table. She pocketed the shells.

In the meantime, Jed was lying there, rubbing his hand on his head, complaining about a headache. He didn't appear to realize he had pulled a weapon on an officer. Or, if he did, he didn't give a damn.

Hedi dropped to her knees and wrapped her arms around the kids.

Pierce took in the scene, and his heart melted. He reached down and belted Jed with his boot. "What kind of a man are you that you reduced your kids to this?" he snapped.

Jed just looked at him with hate in his eyes, but then his gaze fell on his kids bawling all around Hedi.

Pierce could see the sorrow and self-condemnation in the man's eyes. He wasn't just an asshole; he was somebody on a downward spiral. Pierce stepped past and walked to the front door. Sure enough, nearby was a gun cabinet full of weapons. He whistled and spoke over his shoulder. "Hedi, does he have licenses for all of these?"

"Not likely," she said. "I've taken them away in the past, but the sheriff just hands them right back."

He turned to stare at her.

She shrugged. "It won't stop until something really ugly

happens," she said in a low voice.

"Where's the mother?"

"She works at a Laundromat in town," she said. "She'll be home in time to cook dinner. But he's supposed to be looking after these young ones."

"Yeah, right. Find upstanding citizen you got here." He walked back over and crouched beside Jed, who still lay on the ground. "So have you done anything decent for your family in the last couple years?"

Jed looked at him warily. "Who are you?"

"It doesn't matter who I am," Pierce said. "What I will be is your biggest nightmare for the next couple days until I find Salem."

Confusion clouded Jed's gaze. "Salem?"

"Yeah. The best damn dog anybody ever had that apparently this town has done nothing but treat like a piece of shit."

Something flit into Jed's gaze and had him shifting his eyes to the side.

Pierce studied him for a long moment, stood and turned toward Hedi. "I think the dog is here," he said. "I want to take a look."

"Not without his permission," Hedi said firmly. "And he ain't giving it."

He glanced down at Jed, who sneered up at him. Pierce dropped to the ground and grabbed Jed's wrist with his free hand. "You right-handed?"

Fear flared in Jed's gaze. He tried to pull away his hand, but Pierce just crunched his fingers together.

"I want to see if you got my dog," he snapped. And kept squeezing.

"She isn't here. She isn't here," he cried out. "And it

ain't your dog."

"She is now," Pierce said. "Somebody has got to give a damn about her. And, if that ain't you guys, it sure as hell is me."

CHAPTER 3

H EDI STUDIED THE man with the vicelike grip on Jed's hand, watching the hard coldness in his eyes and the panicked look on Jed's face. She stepped closer. "Hey, you need to back down."

Pierce turned slowly to look at her. "Hell no. Jed's a bully, picking on kids, and only understands one thing, and that's dominance."

Even as she watched, he tightened his hand around Jed's fingers and listened to him scream.

Urgently she rushed to his side. "But not in front of the children."

Pierce looked at the children and smiled. "Hey guys, have you seen a big dog around here?"

The oldest one nodded. "Daddy had it for a while. But it took off."

As Hedi watched, Pierce eased up the pressure on Jed's fingers, helping Jed to sit up, but kept a grip on his shoulder where he knew he could render him unconscious if need be. "Any idea where the dog went?"

The little girl shook her head slowly. "He just wasn't here one day."

"*He?*" Pierce asked. "Do you know if it was a boy or a girl dog?"

She smiled, showing the beautiful young woman in her,

if she ever had a life without fear.

"It was a girl dog," she said proudly, as if that was an association she could be a part of. "She was a nice dog too."

"Do you know why she took off?"

Her gaze slid toward her father and then back again, but she didn't say a word. Pierce gripped Jed's collarbone harder and in a low tone said, "I'll owe you for that too then, won't I? You're stacking up reasons for me to teach you a hard lesson."

Jed started blubbering.

"Go easy," Hedi said, with a motion at the children.

Pierce locked gazes with Hedi. "Is there anything you can do about this guy to keep him from scaring the kids?"

"It's hard to do if the sheriff won't back me up," she said in low tone.

Pierce nodded.

"He beats them," she said in a low voice. "Not just his kids but also his wife."

"And he also pointed an armed weapon at you," Pierce said. "In no man's law is that allowed."

"I've tried to pull him in for that before too," she said, "and the sheriff just lets him go."

"And the population around here put that sheriff in power?"

At that, she fell silent.

He looked down at Jed. "Pretty sure you voted for him, didn't you?"

"I'm sure he did," Hedi said with feeling.

Jed just glared at them.

As if not liking the look in Jed's eye—and who would, considering he looked feral—Pierce clamped down even tighter on the muscles behind Jed's collarbone, with Jed screaming like a little girl. Pierce leaned down and whispered in Jed's ear, "I've decided that I'll be around for a long time. If I even hear you have hurt these kids or their mother or even threatened to hurt them, I'll come back and pay you a visit in the dark of night." His voice was soft and deadly. "And you don't even want to think about what I'll do to you if you ever pull a gun on Hedi again."

Fear lit up Jed's eyes as he stared into the cold darkness of Pierce's. And that was one scary gaze. Hedi was stunned. She didn't know who or where Pierce had come from but, not only was this guy completely dominating Jed, Pierce was worried about the condition of the children and herself, even the absent mother. More than that was the fact that Jed was terrified of this man. And that was something she could get behind.

"Kids, can you show me where you last saw the dog?" Hedi tried to move them away from the obvious power play.

The oldest girl walked toward the door, calling to her brother and sisters. The four of them ran outside.

Outside Hedi stopped for a second and took several deep breaths. Every time she came here she knew she was taking her life in her hands. At some point, Jed would go over the line, and she would pay the price. She'd thought for sure it was today. That look in his eyes was just blood-spitting mad.

As she stood here, a little hand slipped into hers. She looked down to see Molly, her eyes still nervous as she crept close and hung on to Hedi's leg. "Is Daddy feeling better now?"

"I think Daddy will feel much better for quite a while," she said. At least she hoped so. As long as he believed Pierce's threat, Jed would behave himself, at least for a bit.

She'd tried to get their mom to leave him, but Jed was

just as much of a threat to her if she lived with him or not. In fact, he threatened to do away with her and take the kids and go visit his grandpappy somewhere in the north country. She didn't even know what that meant, but, as a threat, it was pretty effective.

Molly stepped up onto the porch again to be with her. She leaned up and said, "Do you know that man?"

"No, not particularly," Hedi said. "Why?"

Molly looked back toward the door, where the two men were still in their line of vision. "My dad is scared of him."

"Is that good or bad?" Hedi asked curiously.

"It's good," Molly said, and then she darted toward the barn. "The dog was here."

"Do you know when she came here? Or how she got here?"

"Daddy just said he would keep her for a while. She'd be good for getting meat."

Hedi nodded slowly. "You know that's not a good way to hunt animals, right?"

"There's no good way to hunt animals," Molly said. "But Daddy says we have to have meat, that he doesn't have any money and that we need to eat somehow."

"True enough," Hedi said. "Come on. Show me where she was kept."

She followed the kids toward the barn, hoping it was okay to leave Pierce and Jed alone. Maybe without any women around to see his humiliation, Jed would show a little more fire so Pierce could punch it out of him. She was all about Pierce dominating this drunken excuse for a father and a husband. The problem was, the next time he got a hold of a bottle, Jed would be pretty damn ugly. And, if he remembered this, it would just be a meaner version of pretty damn ugly.

At the barn, the kids led her to a couple dog runs. They were all empty at the moment but large enough to have kept something Salem-size.

"Do you know how long ago the dog disappeared?"

They just shrugged. Time had very little meaning for kids. But it sounded like Jed had had the dog since the dog supposedly escaped from the police yard up until Salem ran away. Which meant that either Ross or Jed was responsible for cutting the fence and letting her out. And that was interesting in itself. Then again the sheriff might have done so himself to get rid of the dog.

"Has your dad had any other dogs?"

The kids shook their heads.

"Has he ever kept any people in the barn?" She didn't know why, but she'd had to ask that question. After all, if Jed abused his wife and four kids, then abused Salem, what's to stop him from branching out, like into human trafficking? That downward spiral Jed was in could lead to all kinds of criminal activity.

The kids shook their heads again.

Hearing their answers, sheer relief washed through her. She still didn't know if Jed was evil through and through or if he was just a misguided soul who had fallen down a deep, dark well of abuse and addiction and was taking out his ills on those he should have loved the most, on those who could have loved him the most. He still had no excuse for abusing his family, then Salem.

Hedi looked around the area. "Looks like the dog would have been quite comfortable here."

"It was nice to see her," Molly said. "I didn't like the way Daddy treated her, and she didn't like Daddy at all."

"I'm sure she didn't," Hedi said.

"Is that man taking the dog away?"

"I think so," Hedi said. "I don't know who she legally belongs to, but I think he has some kind of a claim to her."

"I hope he does then. I liked the dog. I don't want anything to happen to her."

Hedi smiled at the little girl and picked her up, hating that she was out here stumbling around in bare feet. But then, as she looked at the other kids, she saw they were barefoot too. "I should have had you put your shoes on before I brought you outside," Hedi said sorrowfully. "Your feet will get all scratched up."

Molly looked at her in surprise. "Our shoes are only for going to town and for school. We're not allowed to ruin them out here."

"Ah, you only have one pair of shoes each?" she asked.

"Yes," Molly said. "Daddy said we don't have any money."

"No, I imagine it's tough times right now."

Hedi led the way back to the house, an anger burning deep inside. Although it might be tough times, these kids had no shoes, and that asshole of a father had money for booze. And that dropped her back to thinking whether they made moonshine in the proverbial back forty.

She thought they had twenty-acres out here, but it was woodland acres. You couldn't grow anything without bringing in truckloads of good dirt. So all kinds of stuff went on in these back corners that the sheriff's office or the police department never had a chance to see.

As she walked toward the front door, she could hear the two men talking. Jed now stood on his feet, and Pierce faced him, apparently reading him the riot act. But Jed's head was hunkered down, his shoulders were slanted in, and he leaned forward, taking the verbal beating Pierce dished out.

She stopped the kids from going in because she was just too damn happy to see this and didn't want to interrupt Pierce.

When Pierce fell silent, he turned and looked at her through the screen door. He motioned for her to come in. She pulled the door open and stepped in the house, putting Molly on the floor. "Jed, you need to get these kids a second pair of shoes or boots to wear outside."

He lifted his tired gaze and stared at her. "There ain't no money for shoes."

"I heard Jacky down at the gas station was looking for a hand."

Jed's lip curled.

She held up a finger and pointed it at him. "Don't you let your pride get the better of you," she snapped. "A job is a job."

"He won't pay enough to put food on my table."

"He's paying more than doing nothing but sitting here and drinking booze that could have paid for shoes." She studied his gaze to confirm her suspicions. She stepped closer. "Unless you're making it yourself out in the back illegally."

He just raised his eyebrows and stared her down. "We ain't doing nothing like that," he said stoutly.

"Right," she snapped. "Like I believe you."

He gave her an almost injured look, as if to say he was the most innocent man in the world. But no man who beat his wife and kids and a dog was innocent.

She turned to walk back to the front door, then paused and looked at Jed. "Whether Pierce is here or not, the next time you point a gun at me, you better be prepared to shoot it because I'll fire first." And she walked out, letting the door snap closed behind her.

When she heard it open again, she knew it was Pierce. She walked to her cruiser and got in. She didn't give him a chance to speak. She slammed the door shut, turned on the engine and backed out, deliberately avoiding his gaze.

She didn't know why she was being difficult. Part of it was because he'd done something she couldn't do. It was something she was supposed to do as a deputy, but some things the badge just wouldn't change. Jed would never listen to a woman.

And she headed off down the road.

PIERCE WAS IN the truck and on her tail almost immediately. He couldn't get anything else from Jed about where the dog was. The kids had spent a few minutes telling him the dog just disappeared not too long ago. But Pierce knew something was going on when he watched Hedi, the lovely deputy, get in her car and take off. He figured she was either heading back to talk to the sheriff about whatever it was or, better yet, she'd ponder over it a bit herself.

Now he had something to wonder about. It had damn-near broken his frozen solid heart when he saw Jed lift that rifle and point, and then slam it directly against her shoulder. When he found out the damn thing had been fully loaded, he was beyond furious. But she'd stared down Jed, calm and collected as could be. Pierce had seen the fine shimmer of sweat on her forehead and knew she understood just how close she'd come to getting shot today.

Was that what her life was like? Dealing with these kinds of assholes? He remembered the sheriff had just brushed it off, saying Jed was harmless. But nobody who tried to shoot a deputy or even threatened a deputy was harmless.

From the looks of it, the kids were not so much abused as neglected. Then again, some beatings were done where the damage couldn't be seen. Hedi had said Jed was hitting the kids, and Pierce trusted her. Now he had to do something about it. And about protecting the wife too.

But he was here to first follow up on Salem's fate. He wasn't too happy with what he had heard. It sounded like she'd been mistreated for a long time and had done her best to get away from her abusers, like any other animal, human or four-legged.

Up ahead he watched as the deputy pulled off on the shoulder and shut off the engine. He pulled in behind her and hopped out. She didn't get out but sat in the car, having rolled down her window.

"Are you following me?" she asked bluntly.

He grinned. "No, it's the only way back, the direction we came in."

She nodded. "It is. But you don't have to be quite so close. I'm fine, you know?"

He studied her intently for a long moment. "You shouldn't be," he said just as bluntly. "You could have died today."

"It's part of the job." There was a note of fatigue in her voice. "I'm the only one who will talk to Jed."

"None of the other deputies will? Are they men?"

She nodded. "That's one of the sheriff's big beefs. There shouldn't be women deputies. We're all supposed to sit at home and bake apple pies," she snapped, repeating the sheriff's earlier words. "It doesn't matter that female deputies are found the world over. As far as he's concerned, in *his* county, that ain't happening."

Pierce nodded. "It doesn't mean he's right, just means he's an asshole and a sexist. The thing is, guys should go out there, and they should give Jed a good shakedown every time he pulls shit like that. What happens if you tell the sheriff what happened today?"

"He'll say I handled it wrong, and what did I expect? How I couldn't possibly understand what it was like to lose my livelihood and be dependent on a wife." Her tone was dry, but she said it almost in a routine way, as if she'd said it time and time again. Then she had.

"Your sheriff really doesn't like you, does he?"

"He doesn't like very many people," she said. "The fact that I am his deputy is just adding insult to it."

"Then he's an idiot." Pierce's tone was hard. "He needs to move into the new age."

"Maybe," she said, staring out at the countryside around them. "But, just because you and I say so, won't make it happen." She glanced back up at Pierce.

He had to agree. "What do you know about the dog?" he asked.

"Why do you care so much about her?" she countered.

He hesitated, wondering how much he could tell her. Then he realized, no longer being in the military, this wasn't a secret mission. He squatted in front of her door, and she opened it to see him better.

"Salem was a War Dog. She spent a lot of time training. She saved lives in Afghanistan," he said. "We send the War Dogs home with their handlers for a better life. She'd been injured and had a terrible time recovering. Pete was also injured, as you know. Then she lost Pete. Even though he's still alive and fighting the good fight, he can't do it with her at his side. As a general rule, War Dogs are well taken care of, but somehow Salem fell through the cracks. We're not supposed to get attached to our dogs while we're over there, but it's unavoidable. I certainly loved mine, and I know most of the handlers loved theirs. In this case, I was asked to track down Salem when somebody in the division realized Pete couldn't possibly be looking after Salem. She should have been handed to another person capable of looking after her."

Hedi frowned at him. "Seriously, you're from the government?"

"I'm here on the behest of a commander from that department in the military," he said, "but the job came through Titanium Corp, which is a group of former military SEALs now trying to help people like me, and, in this case, dogs like Salem, find a new and better life."

She latched on to what he had accidently slipped out. "Like you?"

He shrugged. "I came stateside almost ready for a metal box," he said. "I spent a long time in a hospital. In the meantime, my beloved wife …" His words carried a cynical tone. "… found somebody better, divorced me, and, in the process, somehow I lost my home and everything else. My dog was killed on the same mission that injured me." His voice halted for a moment. "So I didn't even have the comfort of knowing Trigger was at my side. And, to be honest, like Pete, I couldn't have looked after her for the first while. I was in pretty rough shape."

She nodded slowly. "You look fairly healthy now."

"I am," he said, "or at least as good as I'll get. We received a dozen files of dogs potentially in trouble that had gone missing or were in bad situations. The military didn't know what their fate was, and so they asked Titanium Corp if somebody had time to volunteer to check them out."

"Have you found any of them yet?" she asked.

"We only started a little bit ago," he said. "Ethan, a former K9 trainer, went looking for the first one. He found him guarding a drug lab and being trained to kill intruders." At her gasp he nodded grimly. "And you know what happens to dogs that kill humans." His voice was bleak. "Ethan got there in time to rescue four shepherds from that fate. He has now taken all four on. Plus I believe, from what I last heard, he adopted a fifth one, who just lost her leg and had no place to go and will need special care. He's decided to build his own group of trained dogs."

"Is that what you're looking to do, bring this one back to him?"

Pierce shrugged. "I'm not exactly sure what I'm supposed to do at the moment. The first thing is to get the dog, make sure she's safe and cared for. She saved a lot of lives and spent a lot of years in service for her country. She deserves better than being tossed into this shithole and being used to track down deer, for God's sake. Man's got guns. He should be out there with a hunting license and hunting them humanely."

"It's not even hunting season," she said. "Something else the sheriff doesn't give a damn about."

"Sounds like you need a new sheriff," Pierce snapped.

"We do. Indeed, we do," she said. "But that's not likely to happen anytime soon. Public sentiment has to be swayed."

"Is everybody for the sheriff, or are they all just afraid of him?"

She frowned. "You picked that up pretty fast. I'd say

seventy percent are afraid of him. Of the others, ten percent are for him, like Jed. And the rest just don't give a damn because they don't think it matters what they say or do."

"It sounds like politics everywhere," he said. "Still, that doesn't change the fact the sheriff isn't doing his job. People are getting away with all kinds of criminal acts, and the whole county will end up in a bad way very soon." He motioned back at the house. "Hopefully Jed will lay off the kids and the wife for a while. But nothing will stop a man for long who's hell-bent on destroying himself and the world around him."

"That's too bad," she said. "I was so hoping he would go on the straight and narrow." There was a note of humor in her voice. "You're pretty damn scary when you want to be."

His lips kicked up at the corner. "I can be," he agreed. "When the time warrants it. And I'm wondering what the hell we're supposed to do about that piece of shit sheriff you've got here."

"As soon as you figure it out, you tell me because I haven't a clue."

"How many other deputies do you have?"

"Two. And, before you ask, they're both like him."

"So how did you get the job?"

She rolled her eyes. "The mayor thought it was a good idea, a woman-initiative thing. I think they both thought I'd be stuck at a desk, making coffee for the guys when they came in from their hard work," she snapped. "But, as soon as they gave me the deputy badge, I was the first one out the door, patrolling the trouble spots. I knew what deputies did. I was raised by a sheriff. My dad isn't terribly impressed I'm a deputy, but he's even less impressed with the sheriff who replaced him."

"Why did your dad step down, or was he forced out in an election?"

"Car accident," she said succinctly. "He's better, but he's not 100 percent. He withdrew from his position, which is when they brought in our current sheriff."

"Do you think the voting was fair?"

"They put him in, but I don't think they expected what they got. They should have though. He's been in this community a long time. My father was horrified. He felt for sure the people would have understood and known better, but the sheriff was a smooth talker back then. He doesn't give a shit about being a smooth talker now. He runs this place like he's a god."

"Except he can't seem to keep you in line."

"No. I've placed a couple complaints above his head," she said, "so he's worried about me. He doesn't know how much trouble I'll be for him, so he lets me do my stuff. He rarely calls on me, only sends me out on jobs if he thinks something'll scare me away, instead of jobs he thinks I can handle. Other than that, we try to avoid each other."

"And yet, you followed him down the road coming in the café?"

She nodded. "I did," she said in surprise. "How did you know that?"

"Because I watched you," he said. "Even from where I was having coffee, I could see. But I don't know if you were following him to see what he was up to or if you needed him to see you before you went to Jed's place."

"A bit of both," she said. "I was hoping he'd go give Jed a talking to. When I realized, as usual, he wasn't, I went instead."

"Interesting that he's okay with abusing women and

children. Is he an abuser himself?"

"His wife is dead," she said slowly. "So I don't know. He has no children. I'm not sure he has any girlfriends either. If he does, they're short-term, even possibly by the hour." She laughed. "Listen to me. I'm starting to sound like a real bitch."

"No. You're trying to understand the character of the man who's supposed to be a leader. The one you're supposed to follow into battle," he snapped.

She shook her head. "That I would never do. Call me disloyal if you want, but he's just as likely to lead me into a battle and step out of the way so I take the first bullet."

Pierce stared at her for a long moment. "It's definitely time to do something about him before you do end up with a bullet. Jed looked like he was mighty happy to put one in you today."

"I'm not sure he wouldn't have done it too," she said shortly. She turned in her seat, closed the door, started up the engine and said through the open window, "Try to stay out of trouble." And she drove off.

CHAPTER 4

HEDI SHOULDN'T HAVE told him as much as she had. She didn't know what kind of a man he was, and, with information like that, ... he could get her in a lot of trouble.

She didn't want to work for a man she didn't trust. She didn't want to work for a man she couldn't follow into battle, to use Pierce's term. She could understand his military background. It came out in his words every once in a while.

Her heart ached for Salem. That dog had had a shitty deal once Pete had to go into the rehab center on a permanent basis. She should have done more for Salem, but it wasn't like she had any place of her own to keep her. And, if Salem was as difficult as the sheriff said, Hedi didn't have the training or the know-how to handle her. But maybe Pierce did, and maybe the best answer yet was to have Salem somehow get back into his possession. He hadn't said his orders were official, so she didn't know if he could just take the dog. But, considering the way the dog was being handed around, maybe that was the best answer after all. In this case, she thought, possession was nine-tenths of the law. Maybe that's how Pierce should handle it too.

She finally pulled into the station, parked and walked inside. It was late already; the sheriff was long gone, and so was Roy. That only left Stephen.

He looked up and frowned at her. "Where the hell you

been? I had to do all this paperwork shit myself today."

She just raised an eyebrow. "Oh, poor baby." She left it at that.

Stephen did the least amount of work possible, avoided paperwork whenever he could, but he hated going out on rides and dealing with difficult situations even more. Why he was the deputy, she didn't get. He should have been a librarian or something equally placid.

"Hey, it's not easy sitting here, picking up the reins when everybody else doesn't do anything," he said. "You better be doing your own paperwork for whatever the hell you were up to today."

"I will." She walked to her desk and sat down, logging onto her computer. "I was at Jed's again."

At least he didn't seem to think along the sheriff's line that Jed was harmless. "You know that's just a plain bad situation, don't you?"

"Even more than you know," she said, suddenly weary. She turned to look at him. "If I end up with a bullet between my eyes, you start looking at Jed first, will you?"

Stephen raised his head over the monitors. "That bad?"

"He poked me with his loaded rifle and told me to get the hell off his property," she said, paraphrasing. To be honest she'd been so damn scared she didn't remember his words exactly.

"He pushed you?"

She nodded.

"And you're still standing? He didn't shoot you or any-thing?"

She could hear from the tone of disbelief in his voice that he was confused as to why she was still here, not splattered all over the front of Jed's yard.

"Yes," she said, "I am. His rifle was loaded. He was drunk. And he was screaming at the kids. They're the ones who called me."

"Well, yeah. But you gave them your direct number," Stephen said. "That's what dispatch is for, remember?"

"Yeah? And by the time dispatch gets me on the end of the phone, you know those kids will be dead one day."

Stephen winced. "Unfortunately that's all too possible," he muttered. Stephen had a wife and two kids himself.

As she thought about it, she realized he'd have been a better accountant than anything. He really liked numbers. "Anything happen here this afternoon?"

"Nothing as exciting as your afternoon apparently. The sheriff came back in a pissy mood from his apple pie trip. Don't know what that was all about."

"He met somebody in the restaurant looking for Salem, somebody not taking no for an answer."

"What do you mean?" Stephen frowned.

"Somebody was sent here by the War Dogs division to look for Salem."

Stephen pushed his chair back. "Oh, God." He looked around frantically. "Are we in shit then?"

"Oh, I imagine we're all in shit," she snapped. "Just think about how much that poor dog has been through. Just think about the damn sheriff and how he treated her."

Stephen winced. "He hated that dog."

"And he did what he could to turn her into a mean vicious bitch," Hedi said.

"Well, you couldn't stop him," Stephen said. "Did you expect me to do anything?"

And that was the problem with Stephen. He always took the easy way out.

"Jed apparently had the dog up until a month ago or so, and he was trying to teach it to track down deer out of season. Said he needed the meat so he could live. Then the dog took off one day, and no one has seen it since."

"You mean, to sell the meat so he could buy more booze," Stephen said caustically. "He should be dead from the amount of alcohol running through his veins."

She remembered the yellow tinge to Jed's eyes. "I'm not sure he's far off."

"Hopefully soon," he said, "before Jed beats one of those kids to death, shoots you or that wife of his. That woman is a bloody saint."

"I don't know about a saint," Hedi added, "but she's beaten, downtrodden, terrified of leaving him because he has threatened to come after her and kill them all."

"And he would," Stephen said in a matter-of-fact tone and promptly returned to his monitors and whatever work he was doing.

She stared at him. "And so, like the sheriff, you won't do anything about it?"

His gaze turned hard. "You want to be the cavalry, then have at it. Me? I like my safe desk job."

"You don't have a desk job," she enunciated carefully. "You're a deputy. You're supposed to be out riding with me."

"I go sometimes," he said, "but you don't like doing the paperwork any more than anybody else. Everybody is happy to dump it on me."

"You're more than happy to get out of dealing with con-frontations." On that note she spun around and logged back into her computer.

She wrote up a report, once again on Jed—this time

adding in him pushing her with a loaded rifle. She decided to keep Pierce's name out of the report. She wasn't sure why, but it seemed more prudent to do so. She almost wished he'd go back during the night and haul Jed out into the middle of the woods and pound him into the ground to make him see sense. But Jed would just come back to the house and grab a bottle and upend it all at once, fueling his anger and taking it out on his family.

She did marvel at his liver's resilience. But it had to stop at some point. She'd much rather it was sooner than later.

When she finished her report, she saw Stephen had left without saying goodbye. Only her desk light was on in the main office; the rest were all turned off. "Good riddance," she groaned.

She logged off, grabbed her purse and keys, and headed to the front door. As she locked up and turned to her car, a voice spoke from the darkness. "Are you going home now?"

She turned to see Pierce leaning against his truck. "Jesus, don't do that," she said. "You scared me."

"You've been working in there alone for the last twenty minutes. What's wrong with the men in this town?"

"If you're about to make a sexist comment yourself," she snapped, "I suggest you don't. Besides, Stephen would be useless as a defender or backup. The most dangerous things in his world are paper cuts."

"Is he the admin?"

"No. He holds the same position I do," she said wearily. "He just chooses not to do anything but paperwork." She could hear Pierce swearing steadily and softly under his breath. She gave him a ghost of a smile. "I do that exact same thing many times in a week." She stared off into the distance. "Not sure how much longer I can handle this job. I admit one of the reasons I stay is because I think this town needs somebody who cares. For a little while there, I thought I could change things. But I can't. Not this way at least."

"No, but the town does need you," he said, surprising her. "I'd hate to see you killed on duty by one of those assholes like Jed, but somebody needs to care, and sometimes the only ones who can care are us."

She smiled as she walked to her car. "Where are you staying?"

"Haven't thought about it," he said absentmindedly. He studied the woods behind the sheriff's department. "Where's the compound the dog was held in?"

"It's over here." She detoured to the pen where the dog had been kept. "I used to come out here to talk to her. She accepted my voice and would let me touch her a little bit, but the minute any of the men came toward her, she would get aggressive."

"Great," he said. "That'll make my job harder."

"Yes, it will," she said. "I'm sorry about that. If you're right that Salem was a well-trained dog and came back looking for retirement and a nice dog bed by a fire, she landed in the wrong place."

"I presume the brother is responsible for that?"

"I'd say so," she said steadily. "Pretty sure he lied about the dog bite, and, even if she did bite someone, I'd believe she had good reason. Still, that report had the effect of allowing the sheriff to collect the dog, and then she was *stolen* supposedly as she disappeared from the compound," she said for emphasis. "When I think about it, I think somebody just cut that wire to make it look like she was stolen. And, of course, now all the townsfolk are terrified of her because she's supposedly dangerous."

"Who did she bite again?"

"Jed's brother," she said. "Chester was visiting at the time. He's gone back East now."

"Well, isn't that convenient?"

HE SNORTED AT that. "Doesn't really matter though, does it, because the sheriff wouldn't give a shit, neither would Ross, and I'm sure nobody told Pete anything."

"I'm sure nobody did. I don't think Ross even goes to visit him. It's Pete's house too."

"Seriously? Does Ross look after it, pay rent, anything?"

She shook her head. "Ross doesn't work any more than Jed does. I know they blame everything on the mill that closed down around here, but honestly I think they're just too lazy to find another job." She studied the back compound. "I was delighted when I heard the dog had escaped, until I saw the wires were cut. And then I figured it was some bigger asshole than Ross. He's just lazy. Jed is a mean drunk, and the Billy boys, Billy and Bobby Billy, are downright mean. When that group is together, it's bad news."

"Maybe I'll pay a visit to Pete, see what he wants to do about his house. It might be time to sell it," Pierce said. "I don't know what he can get, but it would help him with his medical expenses and care. Maybe even could get him into a better place."

She stared at him. "You know you'll open a hornet's nest, right?"

He gave her a shadow of a smile. "I hope it's a really big colony when I do." He turned to his truck and hopped in. "Are you okay to go home? Is Jed likely to come after you?"

"He hasn't yet." She got in her car, turned on her engine and headed toward the road.

He watched as she took a left. He waited for a long moment; then he followed her back to the main road. One of the things at the top of his list, besides finding the dog, was solving Pete's problem because that was part of this whole bigger issue.

He remembered what Pete's house had looked like and the land around it. It was a nice place. A small smile formed on his mouth. He picked up his phone and called Badger. "What are the real-estate prices on the outskirts of Fort Collins?"

"Um, I don't know. Let me ask my little crystal ball here," Badger said. "Why?"

"Because Salem has been badly mistreated, taken and dumped from one man to another, incurring more abuse every time. She's currently 'missing,'" he snapped. "Pete's brother has taken over the house but didn't look after the dog, isn't looking after the property, and I'm about to go talk to Pete and see if he needs a hand to maybe get his life back on track."

"You think he wants to sell?" Badger asked as the confusion cleared in his voice. "Or maybe you're looking to buy?"

"What I'm looking for is to make sure Pete is taken care of," Pierce said. "And that asshole brother of his who wouldn't look after Salem needs to be booted off the property."

"Someone will have to," Badger said, "otherwise that brother will just move back home again."

"Let me talk to Pete. I can't imagine the property around here is worth much, but Pete needs what he can get." He hung up on that note.

He headed into Fort Collins and grabbed the first hotel he could find. There he unloaded his bags and laptop and started doing more research. All his shit was in his truck, but he didn't have much. Which was why it seemed odd to all of a sudden consider maybe he should have more.

When he found the telephone number for the rehab place where Pete was, Pierce put in a phone call. Pete wasn't available, but Pierce left a message and said it was about Salem. When his phone rang a half hour later, he smiled to see the number. "Pete, is that you?"

"I got a message," the man said hesitantly. "Who am I talking to?"

"My name is Pierce Carlton of Titanium Corp. I'm here on behalf of the War Dogs Program. We're doing a welfare check on Salem."

There was a hard gasp, and he could hear tears in Pete's voice. "I'd like a welfare check on her myself," Pete said. "My brother told me that she bit somebody, and the sheriff was going to shoot her."

"Apparently she bit Jed's brother. And Ross was not taking care of her in the first place. According to Hedi, he abused her. I know Jed did too. I think Hedi believes the sheriff cut the wire so somebody else could come and get her."

"No," Pete cried out. "Please tell me that's not true. My brother swore he'd look after her."

"What was your brother like before?" Pierce's voice was stern. "Did you really think a leopard would change his spots?"

"I'd hoped so." Pete was almost crying. "I was hoping to come home, but I don't have any money. Ross looks after all of that, and he said I couldn't get the necessary modifications on the property because there just wasn't any money."

"How is he looking after your money?" Anger Pierce hadn't felt in a long time surged through him.

"He pays the bills, handles my money," he said. "It comes in to a specific bank account, and he pays for this place here."

"How long have you been at the center, buddy?"

"Too fucking long," Pete said. "I was doing well in my recovery until I heard I have to stay here."

"That's not necessarily true. I'll do some investigating into your situation."

"You'd help me?" Pete's voice brightened.

"Is your brother paying rent?"

"No, of course not. He's looking after the property for me."

"Exactly what does that mean?"

"Mowing the lawn, taking care of the animals, … just the usual. There's not much population there, so it's not like I can rent it anyway," he said.

"Do you trust him?"

Pete's voice was hesitant. "Not really but I didn't have much choice."

"Do you know how much your pension is?"

Pete named a figure that had Pierce's eyebrows rising. "Your brother said you couldn't get modifications on the house for that kind of money? And that you needed to stay where you are?"

"Yeah. If I can't have the modifications, there's no way to go home. But it's not just the house," Pete said hurriedly. "I have to do some work on the truck too. It's so expensive."

"Yeah. So expensive," Pierce said. "I can do a lot of this kind of work. How about I go to your place and see what it would cost to modify it so you can get a wheelchair in, ensure a bathroom and a bedroom are on the main floor."

There was silence, and then Pete said, "If you could do that, that would be great. But I don't even know you."

"Nope, you don't," he said. "Don't suppose you know an Ethan though, do you?"

"Ethan Nebberly? Trainer from the K9 unit?"

"Yes," Pierce said. "Give him a call and then call me back." And he hung up.

He opened the motel door and stepped out on the long veranda to see where to grab some food. A fast-food joint was across the road. Definitely not his first choice, but, given the circumstances, he had few options. He pocketed his cell phone, grabbed his wallet, locked the door and walked across the street. He ordered a couple burgers and a coffee to go and sat there eating them. They tasted like sawdust, but they were food. As he ate, he wrote notes of what he'd seen and heard. Then he sent them to Badger.

Badger called a few minutes later. "This sounds bad," he said. "It's well out of the parameters of what we asked you to do though."

"The thing is, in order to get Salem's life back on track, Pete needs to come home to look after her."

Badger chuckled. "I guess we didn't give you parameters, and you took the job and ran with it, so we can't argue that. What is it you're thinking you can do? I want to know if anybody else can help. Possibly Kat can get the medical records, see how bad Pete is, see what he needs to become independent."

"He'll talk to Ethan. Then I'll return to his house tomorrow and start measuring to see just what I think will be required."

"I like the sound of that," Badger said. "What do you want to do about his bank accounts?"

"I want them frozen," Pierce said succinctly. "I'm not sure what his brother is up to, but I bet he's been living off of Pete's pension. And probably stocking it away for himself."

"You're not allowed to go in there and beat the crap out of him for that," Badger said.

"You're too far away to stop me," Pierce said, then chuckled. "Still, I think if we were to charge this guy, Pete would have a hard time with that. But we need to find a way to get Pete home and his money back and to stop Ross from taking any more. Can somebody do a check on his bank accounts and see where the money is?"

"You're not asking for much, are you?"

"You've got connections," Pierce said. "You think I haven't been around you guys enough to know that?"

"Well, maybe," Badger said. "We do have some people. We might figure this out."

"There are a couple cops in your group, right? Maybe you could talk to them about what our options are."

"You know what? That's not a bad idea. I think I'll talk to Allison and Jager tonight, see if they have any idea what our options are going forward."

"You should see the law in this town. There's no support here from law enforcement," he said. "The sheriff is an absolute nutjob." He took a few moments to explain everything he'd seen and heard.

"This Jed guy threatened her with a loaded weapon?"

"Yep, whether she told the sheriff about it or not, I don't know. Apparently it's not the first time Jed's gone after her, and the sheriff doesn't give a shit. Jed's a friend of his. And so is Pete's brother. Ross knows there's no one around who'll stop him." Pierce's voice hardened. "Well, *now* there is." He ended the call.

CHAPTER 5

W HEN HEDI WALKED into work the next morning, a
weird silence ran throughout the station. She glanced
from one man to the next, but neither looked her in the eye.
She frowned. "Who died?" she half joked.

Again no answer. Just this weird lack of noise, as if she'd
walked in on a heavy conversation she wasn't supposed to
hear, and everybody shut up when they saw her. But, in that
case, they should have seen her coming because she'd parked
out front. She walked to her desk and logged on to her
computer. Everything appeared normal, but she couldn't get
rid of the niggling sense riding her shoulders.

When the sheriff stepped out of his office and called her,
she frowned. Again she looked at the other two deputies, but
they kept their heads on their paperwork, studiously ignoring
her. That meant something was definitely up.

She grabbed her empty coffee cup, walked to the coffeepot, filled it and headed into the sheriff's office. "Good
morning, Sheriff. How are you?" she said. She deliberately
kept her voice up and cheerful, sitting down opposite him.
"Had a hell of a visit with Jed yesterday."

"That's what I want to talk to you about," he said, his
voice thunderous.

"Oh, good. You're finally on my side and charging him
for assaulting a police officer," she said in excitement. She

knew it would be the opposite of what he planned on doing, but her words stopped him cold.

His mouth worked and then asked, "Did he assault you?"

"He rammed his loaded rifle into my shoulder and threatened me. He pushed me back several inches, and I refused to back down," she said with a hard nod. "I told you that he would cross the line."

"And I told you to leave him alone and to walk carefully around him."

"Sure, except I get there, and all four screaming kids are terrified, and he's running around like a crazy man with that rifle of his," she snapped. She leaned forward. "Did you talk to him?"

Put on the spot, the sheriff shifted papers on his desk. "He called me this morning. He said you crossed the line."

"Yeah? What line was that?" she asked. "Responding to a 9-1-1 call from a little girl?"

At that, the sheriff looked in the direction of dispatch on the other side of the wall. He couldn't confirm or deny what she'd said because, of course, he had no fricking clue. "You didn't mention anything about a 9-1-1 call when we were at the coffee shop," he snapped. "You said you were going up there because one of the girls had called you. Little girls do that." His voice turned snide. "They're weak and whiny, and they don't know how to suck it up."

"No child should have to see their father shooting up the house in front of them. He's done it many times—you know that." Her tone was cool, her back rigid.

She needed a solution to purge this bloody office and wasn't sure how to get it done. She had talked to her father about it last night, and he'd agreed to contact some people he knew, but the wheels turned slowly when it came to elected officials, and the sheriff had been running this town for way too long.

"What else did he say?" she asked in a conversational tone. "Or will you talk to him more about it when you bring him in?"

He glared at her. "You know you have this job only because I gave it to you, right?"

She tilted her head to the side. "Partially yes. I'm also the only one who goes out and handles anything in the field," she snapped. "Stephen is great for paperwork, but you know as well as I do that he's no good in times of trouble."

The sheriff's lip curled. "But there's nothing wrong with Roy."

"Nope, nothing wrong with him at all." In her mind she added, *There's nothing right about him either.*

Roy picked and chose where he went and what he wanted to do. Most of the time, he just wanted to hang around with pretty girls downtown. He called it citizen's watch. She had another name for it. Roy was forty, always leering at her, and there was something extremely lecherous about everything he did. But he never, as far as she knew, crossed the line, and that made a difference. It was one thing to be slime, but it was another thing to be a complete sleazebag.

"You shouldn't arrest Jed without backup."

He started to bluster.

She held her ground. And waited.

"You know I'm not arresting him," the sheriff said. "He had a bad day, that's all."

"Did he call you this morning?"

"I said he did, didn't I?" The sheriff growled. "I'll talk to him again. You stay away from him."

"I'll stay away as long as he stays away from those little girls," she said, "and his wife. And any other godforsaken animal, two-legged or four." She stood, marched to the door and turned. "Make sure you don't get caught up in his garbage because you know this town will only stand for so much. The minute he really hurts someone, and people find out you just sat by and let him get this bad ..."

He rose and leaned over his desk, snapping like a turtle. "And who do you think will tell them that? You?"

She gave him a hard look. "Hell yes, me. And my father. Do you think I haven't told him what the hell's going on? And what about Roger? He might not be a deputy anymore, but he was for twenty-plus years. Do you really think they won't start telling the world just how you're running this town? And letting child abusers and wife abusers get away with that kind of shit?"

She didn't wait for an answer. She opened the door and stepped out, closed it and leaned against it for a long moment because it was the one place the other two deputies couldn't see her.

She stared down at her hands, angry that they were shaking. She shouldn't be upset from the confrontation; she should be priding herself on having had it. It was hard to deal with. This office was a pain in the ass actually. But there was only so much she could fight. She'd tried to contact as many people as she could about the abuses, but what did you do when nobody backed you up?

Taking several deep breaths, she realized she'd left her coffee cup inside. Whatever. She walked to the pot, grabbed a clean mug, filled it, then she went to her desk and sat down without saying a word to either man. She could feel their glances, but she didn't look up. She answered several emails and checked the report she'd written yesterday.

They were barely adjusting to a digital system. The sheriff still wanted handwritten notes, but she kept everything digital, just in case somebody decided to doctor her reports. A practice she'd started a long time ago when she realized only shit was going down here. Because she had no place to submit them, she sent herself a copy and a copy to her father, in case something happened to her, which, after a conversation with her father last night, she realized was a distinct possibility. It would be an accident, she was sure. She'd die in the line of duty, probably from something stupid, like shooting herself with her own gun, if the sheriff wrote up the report.

She printed off the report she had written yesterday and went over it with her pen. Nobody had seen it but her. When she was satisfied it was fine, she slipped it into Jed's file and put it away. Then she wrote herself a small note and stuck the sticky on her monitor to check that the report was still there at the end of the day because she was damn sure somebody who'd been watching her will let the sheriff know, and he was likely to destroy it.

Jed's file was awfully skinny. But she kept copies of everything she had dealt with online, just in case. She didn't want a prosecutor saying Jed was a first-time offender and just give him a slap on the wrist. It was all she could do to sleep at night these days, thinking about those little kids ending up dead, and Jed taking them out back and burying them six feet deep, telling the sheriff some asshole kidnapped them. The sheriff would probably just stand there for a long moment, chewing his gum, as if deciding whether it was worth making up a report and chasing down this unnamed person. And probably choosing it wasn't worth losing an inch off his fat ass and subsequently closing the case.

She hated that this was what she was working with—hated that this was what her badge stood for because it didn't. It wasn't what she stood for, and it was her badge, damn it.

And again she felt helpless, her mind returning to Pierce. She didn't think he'd ever felt helpless. Something about him told her that he'd deal with this, one way or another. She'd heard both hero stories and horror stories about military life.

If he'd been subjected to any of the nightmares she'd heard about, no wonder he'd learned coping skills. But he didn't seem to have any of that ingrained anger she'd seen in a lot of people. Pete himself had gone from being angry to being despondent, as if working through the various stages of grief.

He'd told her once that he was still grieving for what he used to be. He hadn't come to terms with the man he currently was. She'd hoped he would see what he could become, but he was still stuck in the here and now of broken bones and missing limbs and a life that would never be fully realized, not as far as he was concerned.

She didn't know what Pierce's story was, but she could already see the kind of man he was. She just worried he was too high-strung and would cross the line, like Jed had. There was something about men like that. You just didn't quite know when they would explode.

But whatever Pierce was doing now, he was doing from the heart, because nobody else seemed to care about this dog, and that was just wrong.

She was a huge animal lover herself. She had tried hard to get to know Salem, but Salem was already in hate mode by the time Hedi had gotten around to trying to be friends. She only hoped, given enough time, Pierce might find the dog.

Salem had been everything to Pete. Hedi had even seen him bawling as he left because the dog couldn't go with him. She wished there was a way to reunite the two, but just wishing it didn't make it happen; otherwise she would have wished that sheriff away a long time ago.

PIERCE ENTERED THE rehab center and walked to the reception area. He looked around with interest. He'd been in a couple himself but always on a short-term basis. He asked the receptionist where Pete was.

She frowned. "He's taken a turn for the worse." Her voice was quiet. "He can't have any visitors today."

Pierce winced. "I'm sorry to hear that. Maybe leave a message I came to visit."

She gave him a notepad, and he wrote down his name and number.

With a nod of thanks he turned and stepped outside. He had no doubt Pete's downturn was based on Pierce's phone call last night, and that shouldn't be. Pete had enough things in his life to deal with, just getting back on his feet, without having to worry about what happened to his brother and his dog.

Pierce hopped back into his truck and headed back the way he'd come. It had been an hour and a half one way this morning just to get here. Next he'd go to Pete's house, where Ross was effectively squatting.

When Pierce got within about ten minutes of Pete's

place, he pulled off on the side of the road and checked his messages. And, sure enough, there was one. He hit Dial, and this time Pete answered. His voice was quaking slightly. "Pete, how you doing? I heard you didn't have a great night," Pierce said, his voice calm, steady.

"I heard you came by this morning," Pete said. "I'm sorry I missed you."

"I might have a chance to get up there again," Pierce said. "Just thought I'd stop in when I was close."

"Will you do anything about my brother?"

"I'll have a talk with him," Pierce said. "Is there anything you want me to do about him?"

"I had a conversation here with a couple guys, and they think he's probably stealing from me." Pete's voice was heavy. "The doctor said there's no reason I couldn't come home if some modifications were done and if I had some help."

"I think that's a great idea," Pierce said. "The question then is whether you have the money to make that happen."

"Yeah," he said, "that's partly it. I do get a decent pension, and I have my medical expenses covered. The property doesn't have a mortgage, so I was kind of half hoping that maybe ..." His voice dropped off, and he hesitated.

"That maybe what?" Pierce asked as he looked around the area. Not another vehicle had been on the road since he had turned onto it. "Your place is a little isolated, isn't it?"

"It is," he said. "That's the way I used to like it. It'd be kind of nice to have somebody living close by now though. I do have neighbors to a certain extent," Pete added hurriedly. "But they're not necessarily the best kind."

"Meaning that, when a guy gets into trouble, they're not there for you? Not talking about Jed, are you? I haven't even met his brother."

"You're not missing much," Pete said. "They laughed at me when I said I was going into the military, that I wanted to serve my country. And they laughed when I came home in pieces too," he said.

Anger speared through Pierce. "They laughed, did they? Maybe they should have done some time overseas. You and I both know what it was like. I came back mostly in one piece, but I was still in recovery for a long time. You need to focus on getting well. I'll go talk to your brother and take a good look at your house. I just need your permission to go inside and to take some measurements and just to see what your options are."

"You have my permission," he said. "No matter what Ross tells you, that's my house. I haven't signed the title to him."

"I hope not," Pierce said. "And hopefully your brother hasn't forged signatures."

He heard Pete's gasp.

"I'm not saying he did," Pierce rushed to say. "Are there any public health nurses around here, or anybody who could come in on a whenever-needed basis?"

"No," Pete said. "Almost everybody works in Fort Collins or elsewhere."

"Or they don't work at all I gather, now that the mill shut down."

"Exactly," he said.

"Pete, did you have a girlfriend before?"

"I did, yeah." His voice brightened. "We used to call her Smelly"—he chuckled—"but her name is Smelina. It's a Ukrainian name that the kids shortened to Smelly. Now she's Lina."

"I'm sure she prefers that."

"True," Pete said with another chuckle. "We were going out before I headed into the military, but, after my accident, well, I haven't had anything to do with her."

"Because of you or because of her?" Pierce asked.

"What do you mean?"

"Meaning, did she not want to see you because of your condition, or did you stop seeing her because of your condition?"

There was a hard silence, and then Pete said, "You don't pull any punches, do you?"

"Nope. I don't, and I got no patience for it. My wife divorced me and took my house and everything I owned while I was undergoing surgery," Pierce said. "So I understand either way. But, before I meet Lina, I'd like to know."

"It was me," Pete rushed to say. "She's very active. The last thing she needs is somebody like me saddled at her side."

"I think you are supposed to give her that choice," Pierce said, "not make that decision for her."

"Sometimes we have to make decisions for others," Pete said, "because they don't know enough to make an informed choice."

"Meaning, you didn't let her see how bad it was and the modifications you'd need to have a relationship with her."

"Something like that." Pete's voice grew stronger. "I don't know what kind of physical condition you ended up in, but I'm in rough shape. I wouldn't put that on anybody."

"I know you don't believe it," Pierce said, "but the human body really can heal." And on that note he hung up.

He'd heard and seen an awful lot of guys just like Pete walk away from everything they knew because they figured they were less than a whole person, thinking it was a kindness to walk away from their former relationships. And sometimes they were just too angry, not ready to deal with the fact that their life had changed and not able to believe a partner could live with it. So much anger led to a lot of violence, harsh words said that could never be taken back. It sucked all around, but it happened.

He turned the truck engine on again, tossing the phone beside him, and drove until he saw the driveway that went to Ross's place. ... Pete's place, he corrected because Ross liked to think it was his place, but it wasn't. It was Pete's.

As Pierce drove up, he took note of the driveway. Pete would need a vehicle modified so he could drive with his hands, not his feet, and to get a wheelchair in and out of. He thought of Kat when he thought of prosthetics. Pete's medical records would determine what she could do for him.

Pierce pulled up to the front of the house and parked, thinking there should be a garage. Right now there was just dirt, gravel, rocks, a bit of a garden and some steps. But there was lots of room to throw up a ramp.

He hopped out, grabbed a notebook and pen from his glove box, took his phone again and walked toward the front steps. Using his phone, he took several pictures from both angles where a ramp could be built. There was no need to make a big deal out of it; it was only four steps. A ramp wouldn't be a problem, and, once Pete got up those four steps, there was a huge wide veranda. It wasn't a narrow one, barely enough room for a chair. This one was big enough for a table and a couple chairs, which meant the wheelchair could turn around and move in and out. He studied the front door and then said out loud, "That would need to be changed."

"Hey, who are you, and what are you doing?" called out

a man from deep inside the house.

Pierce ignored him, measured off the door and took a solid look at the outside. "Definitely need to have double doors that open at the same time. Certainly couldn't do with a thirty-two-inch exterior door. Why would anyone put such a small exterior door on? Should have been a forty at least." He jotted down more notes, took pictures and measurements. A big window was to the side of the door. He figured, if the window came out, a nice big double set of doors could go in.

As he wrote down notes, the door pulled open, and Ross glared at him sleepy-eyed, his hair still tousled in all directions. Pierce looked at him and said, "Hey. Did I wake you?"

"Yeah, you woke me," Ross snapped. "What the hell are you doing back here?"

"Were you working last night? Sorry. I'm not used to people sleeping this late," Pierce said, making a point to check his watch. It was well past eleven. "But then I guess night shift really sucks, doesn't it?"

"I wasn't working. Not that it's any of your business." He looked at the notepad and pen in Pierce's hand. "What are you doing?"

"Taking notes on modifications for Pete. I'm glad you're up. I need to get in the house anyway." And he stepped inside, not giving Ross a chance to argue.

"What are you talking about? Pete is in rehab, and that's where he'll stay," Ross said. "No way he can come back home."

"Why is that?" Pierce asked as he studied the inside of the door frame. He could definitely double the size of the door by taking that window out. He stepped back and took a picture of it.

"Stop that," Ross said. "You've got no business in my house. Pete can't come home because he's too injured."

"Pete is healing." Pierce turned to look at him. "I've talked to him several times."

"So what? He ain't coming home, no way. That ain't happening." Ross snorted and picked up a pack of cigarettes. He lit one and took a deep drag on the filter end. Within seconds he blew it out.

Pierce could see almost a calm come over him. "You're pretty addicted to those, aren't you?"

Ross raised an eyebrow. "None of your business."

"Nope, not my business that you're killing yourself. Of course it is now that you're smoking inside in front of me, but hey …" Pierce turned and moved off down the hallway.

He measured the width of the hallway, happy to see it was plenty wide for a wheelchair. It might be one person at a time, but the wheelchairs these days were pretty high-end machines. He took the hall down to what appeared to be a large bedroom. He suspected Ross had come stumbling out from there and assumed he wouldn't be impressed to hear the latest plans.

"What the hell are you doing?" Ross roared. "Get out of my bedroom."

"This is the master bedroom, isn't it?" Pierce asked, feigning innocence.

Ross frowned at him. "Yeah, of course it's the master bedroom. And I'm the master of the house."

At that, Pierce straightened. "This is Pete's house."

"It is, but my brother ain't never coming back. Did you hear that? That makes me the master of the damn house," he said belligerently.

Pierce reached up and poked him in the chest. "This is

Pete's house. This is Pete's master bedroom. Pete is coming back to sleep in his master bedroom. Got that?" And he poked him with every word he said.

He had Ross stepping halfway down the hallway, and then Pierce turned back into the master bedroom.

As he stood here, he looked at the entranceway, not liking the size of the door. Somehow the hallway looked like it had narrowed slightly. Out came his trusty tape measure, and he sized up the entranceway.

In the meantime, Ross came back in. "You've got no fucking business being here," he snapped.

At that Pierce pulled out his phone and called Pete. When he answered, he said, "Hey, Pete, I'm putting you on speaker." He watched the color disappear from Ross's face. "Your brother says it's his house, and I have no business taking measurements."

Pete's voice came out of the speaker, gaining strength with every second. "Ross, you there?"

"Yeah, I'm here. What the hell's going on, man?"

Pierce was happy to hear Ross sounding like a whiny child.

"Pierce is there to take some measurements to see just what kind of money is needed to make modifications so I can come home again," Pete said happily.

"Hey, man, I know that's a dream for you, but it's a pipe dream. Remember there's just no money."

At that Pierce smiled at him. "Yeah, we'll talk more about that."

Ross looked at him, and Pierce could see a bead of sweat breaking out on his forehead. "There ain't nothing to talk about, Pete. You know that. You know there's no money."

"I'm just trying to figure out why there's no money,"

Pete said. "I know how much money was in that account, and I've got the accountants taking a look at it to see if we can make this happen."

"Yeah, but I had to fix a few things here," Ross whined. "And I can't live here for nothing."

"No, absolutely not," Pierce said. "So you're looking after this place. What's that worth? A couple hundred bucks a week?"

"At least," he said. "I gotta make sure nobody breaks into the place and causes damage," Ross blustered, then straightened, as if feeling like he was on better ground. "If we'll start looking at that, Jesus, my brother owes me a couple grand for being here."

"Just a couple grand?" Pierce asked. "How long have you lived here?"

"I don't know. It must be about, maybe not quite a year. What do you think, Pete? How long has it been since you went in there?"

"It's been just over six months," Pete said, his tone wry. "I can see you moved in quite nicely, but it's only been six months, bro."

"Feels longer," Ross said. "So six months, you know, that's like twenty-five hundred bucks."

"Sure, but if you, as a renter, look at the rental stats around here, I understand that places go for about five hundred a month, and a whole house goes for about eight hundred. Eight hundred times six is four thousand eight hundred. So by my calculations, you still owe Pete about twenty-three hundred. You only worked off half the rent."

Silence.

Finally Ross blubbered away. "Hey, Pete, what the hell is going on here?" He kept walking, pacing back and forth, sucking on a cigarette like a drowning man.

Not wanting Pete to back down, Pierce said, "Pete, I'll call you back in a few minutes." He hung up and pocketed the phone, going back to looking at the measurements of the bedroom. "This is a nice-size room," he commented out loud. "It's definitely big enough for a wheelchair."

"Man, Pete can't be out here alone," his brother said. "It's not good for him."

"Yeah? Why is that?" Pierce measured the room, just so they had the basics for when they needed them.

He walked into the en suite bath and immediately knew the door would need to come off. Thankfully there was room on either side. They could just take out the door and leave it open.

He wandered through the old-fashioned bathroom, thinking out loud, "This is where the money will go."

"I told you there's no way we can modify it enough for Pete to come home."

Pierce turned to look at Ross, who appeared to be feeling better at that news. "What's the matter? Afraid you'll find yourself out on the street?"

Ross frowned at him. "You're making yourself a lot of enemies. I want my brother home as much as the next man, but not if it'll mean another failure for him."

"It's only a failure if you don't try," Pierce snapped back at Ross. "You're sitting here, living high on the hog in your brother's place without doing anything to give back. If we find out you've taken any of his money, you can bet *out on the street* will be the least of your problems."

"What the hell are you talking about?" he asked. "You don't know nothing about my money."

Pierce just snorted. "Let me put it this way. Every *gov-*

ernment-issued penny Pete had in that bank account better have one hell of an explanation if it's not there, or you'll find yourself in jail."

"Ha. The sheriff ain't doing nothing," Ross said. "We're buddies, and he knows I need money to live."

"Yeah? Did you pay him with any of Pete's money?" He watched something cross in Ross's gaze. And he nodded to himself. "You do realize Pete is a vet, right? He gets special privileges, and, when he needs a lawyer, he gets a lawyer."

Pierce didn't know for sure that the government would provide an attorney, but he knew plenty of guys who would pitch in and help out a veteran like Pete for free if it came to that. If his brother was stealing from him while he was in a rehab center, a lot of guys would come and move Ross out and dump him several counties over, then come back and fix up Pete's place for him. "That's pension money, and, if you're stealing that …" Pierce just shook his head. "You ain't going to like jail much. And it ain't going to be down here at the county lockup. This will be big-time. Actually it'll be hard time." His voice held a word of warning. "So, before I get to checking Pete's bank account and making sure everything is kosher, you better make sure every penny is back in there."

Ross's face turned white.

Pierce looked at his watch. "You got four hours."

Ross started blustering.

"I said, *four hours*," Pierce stated, his voice hard, cold. "I've already got people looking into this, but I'll give you four hour's grace to make sure every goddamn penny is back in Pete's account."

"I can't," Ross whined. "I had to pay the utility bills."

"Yeah, you did, and maybe the taxes, depending on

when they came due. And maybe the house insurance, depending on when that was due. But there had better be an invoice and a receipt for every penny you took."

"I had to have food," he whined. "He owed me for looking after this place. I had to buy groceries. And gas ..." Ross wrung his hands.

Pierce stared at him in disgust. "You heard me. Four hours. A full accounting of every penny and all the proper receipts. And there sure as hell better be an awful lot of receipts in your hands. I suggest you run along and take care of that because, in four hours I'll come knocking, and you'd better have that ready. Now, you're stopping me from doing my work. Get the hell out of here."

He waited until Ross returned to the living room, figuring Ross wouldn't do what he was told. Instead he was probably making some calls. Pierce'd bet five bucks that Ross was calling the sheriff first, then Jed next.

Pierce checked his watch and wondered how long he had before the cavalry showed up to defend Ross. Pierce figured maybe thirty minutes, possibly an hour, not more.

Pierce grabbed his tape measure and headed into the bathroom. He'd like to see this room completely gutted and start from scratch. With all the measurements down, he turned and walked back to the living room.

He wandered the space, realizing this was an older house with lots of rooms, lots of walls, whereas he preferred the open concept, which would be much easier for wheelchair adaptation too. But it was post-and-beam construction. A lot of these walls looked to have been put in afterward, which meant they could also come out.

He took more photographs, wandered around, then headed for the kitchen. In order for Pete to be independent, he needed access to the kitchen and the room to work in it. Pierce winced when he saw it. It wasn't that it was bad; it was just old, and it was tiny. Back to that *whole walls coming out* thing.

He took more measurements, and an idea started to form about how the kitchen should be. He'd always loved cabinet working and carpentry. Remodels were just part of life as far as he was concerned. He'd grown up with a father who was in real estate, and they used to buy and fix up homes and sell them. He'd learned a lot, and he was grateful for every lesson because he would need every one of them here and now. He might find a few local people to help; otherwise he would have to bring in some specialized guys to do the work, and that would get pricey.

He opened the fridge and saw three-quarters of it was full of booze. In disgust he slammed it shut and checked out the plumbing under the sink. It was still copper piping, which said an awful lot about the age of the house too.

"Well, Pete, it will take some money, but we can do a lot on a little."

From the kitchen was a single glass door that opened up onto a deck. He popped it open and looked at the glass door and wrote down another note. It had to be wider, and a ramp was needed to get in and out. The damn threshold was raised, so it would be hard to get the chair's wheels up and over it. This was a shitty job. It should have been put in flush.

He stepped out on the deck and walked the back of the house, taking pictures as he went. There was no railing, but it was wide enough, and stairs were at both ends. The stairs could come out, and ramps could go in, so that was a pretty minor job too. He headed back inside and took a look at the staircase going up. Depending on what Pete wanted to do, the stairs could stay, and an elevator could go in.

As he walked around the side, moving toward the front of the house, he heard the sounds of a vehicle coming, then another and another. He gave a grim smile, tucked his notepad and pen inside his pocket, picked up his phone and dialed. "How you doing, Pete?" he asked as soon as Pete answered.

"I'm doing okay. What do you think of the house?"

"Definitely needs some work done to accommodate you," he said. "The en suite bathroom is likely the biggest cost. The kitchen is a bit small too. But it won't be impossible to do."

"Well, that's good news," Pete said with relief. "It depends on the money then, doesn't it?"

"Depends on how much money you've got and how much help we can rustle up to make some of these changes, also on your mobility." He stood at the front door. "Your brother has called the cavalry too."

"He's what?" Pete yelled out in alarm. "What are you talking about?"

"Pretty sure he's got the sheriff and Jed and God-only-knows-who-else coming down here to have a talk with me and to try to run me off your place."

"Jesus, that's not good," Pete said, sputtering. "I'm getting off the phone, and I'll call you some help." And just like that he hung up.

Pierce laughed. He walked to his truck, pulled out his handgun from the glove box and put it in his shoulder holster he wore underneath his overshirt. Then he walked back to the front steps as the vehicles pulled up and parked. He looked at the sheriff who hopped out and walked toward him, shifting his belt up over his gut. "Sheriff, good to see you again," he said.

"What's this I hear about you running Ross off?"

Pierce raised an eyebrow. "I didn't say anything about running Ross off. I said his brother was looking for an accounting of what kind of work he'd done and how much money he'd spent in the time he's been gone because Pete is on his way back home soon and needs a certain amount of money to make changes on his property."

The sheriff frowned. "What? Pete is coming back?"

"Yeah, Pete is coming back," Pierce said. "We've been back and forth on the phone all day. I talked to him about the various changes required on his house." He launched into an explanation on how he will put a ramp in and double up the front door so the wheelchair could fit.

He turned with a big smile and said, "The bedroom is fine. The hallway is fine, of course. For whatever reason, Ross moved into Pete's bedroom." He shot the sheriff a disgusted look. "Not like there aren't bedrooms upstairs he could have used without trying to move in on his brother's property and take over like he did."

Before Ross could argue, Pierce launched straight back into an explanation of how he will change out the single glass door in the kitchen so it too was a double door and to cover up that bit of a threshold lip so Pete could get out on the deck and then put a ramp around the back.

The men just stared at him.

He looked at them all. "Aren't you guys Pete's buddies?"

Jed just kind of looked down at the ground, and the sheriff ran his hand across his mustache a couple times.

"Are you or are you not his buddies?" Pierce asked, his tone turning hard with a deadly backlash to it.

Jed looked at him and said, "Ross is my buddy."

"I see," Pierce said, crossing his arms over his chest. "So you don't want the owner of the house—who has gone to war, fought for you and your country, been injured, been in recovery all this time—to come back to what's rightfully his?"

Jed had the grace to turn a ruddy red. He backed up a couple steps and spat on the side of the driveway.

Pierce turned his gaze to the sheriff. "And what say you, Sheriff?"

The sheriff pulled the hat off his head and ran his fingers through his hair. "Well, I've known Pete a long time."

"I'm sure you'll tell me that he's a good man," Pierce said. He watched another car come down the road toward them. It was a deputy's vehicle, and he was pretty darn sure it was Hedi.

The sheriff nodded. "He is a good guy. But I understood he's a cripple."

Pierce's eyebrows shot up. "A cripple? What the hell are you calling Pete a cripple for?" He turned on Ross. "Is that your words? Would you disrespect your brother like that?"

Ross opened his mouth and then snapped it shut. "I didn't say he was a cripple."

"I'd be very unhappy to hear you call him that," Pierce said. "That man needs the help of his friends, and I'm still waiting to see it."

"What's this got to do with you anyway?" Jed said.

"I went and fought for my country too, so Pete and I are brothers-in-arms," Pierce said with a half-smile and a hard gaze. "I do a lot of remodeling. So I'm here to help Pete get back into his house. You don't want to see a man like that stuck in an institution, do you? Not when he can live comfortably in his own home."

"I mean, if he's dragging shit bags and crap like that," Jed said, "maybe that's where he belongs."

Pierce snorted. "You know what? I wouldn't be at all surprised if he doesn't come back walking on his own two feet." He kept his tone very low.

Just then the deputy's vehicle pulled up and parked.

"That'd be a fine thing to see," the sheriff said. "Pete is a good man. What happened to him was hard." He turned to look at his deputy and frowned. "What's she doing here?"

"She's here at my request," Pierce said cheerfully. He lifted a hand. "Hey, Hedi. Glad you could make it."

She flashed him a confused look, then walked closer.

He didn't give her a chance to speak. "I've been talking to Pete," he said, "and the good news is, I think we can get his house fixed up so he can get home. It'll take some money and lots of volunteer hours, but I'm pretty sure his buddies here can give us a hand." He waved a hand at the two men standing in front of him.

Hedi's eyebrows rose.

He could see the humor flash across her face before she managed to school her features. "Isn't that right, Jed?" Pierce said. "I know you said you were Ross's buddy more than Pete's, but you know Ross will be here helping out too."

"Like hell I am," Ross snapped. "I can't swing a hammer."

"Everybody can swing a hammer," Pierce said coolly. "Just not everyone can swing it well. And you're not paying Pete any rent, so living here free of charge, spending your brother's money, free and clear without his permission, so I'm sure you'll want to do something to help pay him back for his generosity." Pierce made sure he injected just the right amount of scorn so Ross would stand up and do what was right. Pierce's voice snapped across the silence. "Right?"

Ross spat on the ground and shot Pierce a disgusted look. "It ain't none of your business."

"I'm moving in," Pierce said, "with Pete's permission. So you're either staying here and helping out, or you're getting the hell off this place right now."

Silence whistled across the group.

CHAPTER 6

HEDI COULDN'T BELIEVE it when she got a garbled message from her father to *Get the hell over here*. She knew he was coming too, as well as Roger and a couple other guys. Pete had sent out a call of distress to the old guard, and they'd all taken up the call. But she was the closest and the most available, so she was here first. And just listening to Pierce set down the other men was something to see. She wished she'd been here from the beginning.

"That's great news," she said to Pierce warmly. "I can't wait to see Pete again. He's a good guy." She looked at the front door. "I guess this will all have to change."

Pierce stepped up and explained how he would take out the window and put in a double door that opened both ways.

She nodded approvingly. "He'll need a ramp, and I guess bathroom and kitchen modifications. All that takes money and manpower. And Pete has his pension, with his medical treatments paid for, so there should be lots there for him." The silence behind her got even more awkward. She spun around and looked at the three men, her gaze landing on Ross. "Right, Ross?"

He looked at her resentfully. "Costs money to live here."

She narrowed her gaze. "It might cost a *little* bit of money to live here ..." Her voice was gentle and calm. "... but if a large amount of Pete's pension money disappeared, that would be theft."

Ross straightened his back and glared at her, then looked at the sheriff and back at her again. "Sheriff, you won't let her talk to me like this, are you?"

She turned and glared at the sheriff.

He stared back at her balefully.

That in itself was a shift. She wondered when that had occurred. Then she realized it was in the force of the man in a black truck.

"Ross already knows his clock is ticking away on that." Pierce's voice remained calm and cool as he crossed his arms over his chest and leaned against the front door frame. He looked down at his watch. "By the way, Ross, you're down to three hours now."

Ross spluttered, then snorted and walked back inside. He went to slam the front door, but Pierce's boot was in the way. Ross turned and said, "You're not moving in. You get the hell out of my house."

"But it's not your house," Pierce said.

"How the hell do you know?" Ross snarled. "It's my house if I want it to be my house. You get the hell out of here."

Hedi was shocked. "Hey, what are you talking about, Ross? This is Pete's house. You've been living here for a few months, but you don't just get to move in and take over like it's yours. Pete's making modifications, and he's coming home."

"You believe this snake here?" Ross sneered. "Of course you would. You're nothing but a woman. You'll probably spread your legs for smack."

She hadn't even processed his words before Ross lay flat

on the ground between her and Pierce.

Pierce reached down and, with one hand, grabbed a handful of shirt, lifted Ross up, dragged him out on the deck and plunked him down. "Don't you ever talk to a woman like that again while I'm around." His voice was hard. "The fact that she's a law enforcement officer, who you obviously have zero respect for, is a really bad sign, not to mention her boss stood here and let you treat her like that. But as for me? Nobody treats a woman like that. Now you got twenty minutes to get your shit packed up and get the hell out of here."

"Or what?" Ross said, struggling to his feet, wiping the blood off his cheek. "The sheriff is here. He'll back me up."

Just then three more vehicles pulled into the yard. The sheriff spun around, took one look and said, "Shit."

Ross sputtered, "What ... what ... what's the matter?" And then he saw four men hop out of the newly arrived vehicles.

Hedi walked over and said, "Good timing, Dad." Hedi studied her father. He wore a brushed cotton T-shirt that said he still worked out on a regular basis, plus dark blue jeans, cowboy boots that were cut properly, and a walk, not a swagger, that said this man had seen it all, done it all, and was comfortable doing it all over again. She loved that about him. He'd been a great father and still was her biggest supporter.

Pierce nodded his head. "Good evening. I'm Pierce."

Her father nodded. "My name's Jessie. Glad to meet you." He looked at Ross. "What's this I hear about you not wanting to vacate Pete's house?"

Ross looked to the sheriff. "Sheriff, you can't let them do this to me."

The sheriff lifted his hat again to rub his head. "Well, now this is a bit of a mess up."

"No mess up at all," Pierce said. "Sometimes, when you can't do the job yourself, your friends have to take out the trash." He turned his gaze on Ross. "I mean it. You got twenty minutes, buddy."

"That's not fair. I don't have to leave."

"If you won't help do the work and help make up for the rent money you took from Pete, you're damn right you have to leave. And you're still on a clock for that other accounting problem you have."

Ross gave him a haunted look and stormed inside.

Jessie laughed. "Nice to see you around town, Pierce. We need a few more men like you."

"We need a few more men like you too," Pierce said. "I hope you guys heard from Pete. Did you?"

"Yeah. He called not too long ago, said you were here creating a ruckus."

"You can say that again," the sheriff snarled. "Looks like you don't need me after all." He walked to his car and turned. "I'm heading back to the office." He hopped in, and he drove away.

Hearing the sound of a vehicle, Ross came back outside. When he saw the sheriff leave, he looked like he wanted to cry.

Pierce turned to him. "If you thought the sheriff would back you up, you're dead wrong. In this case, the law is on Pete's side, not yours, and you're down to twelve minutes."

Ross went back inside.

Hedi said, "You'll really make him leave?"

"Oh, yeah, I'll make him leave. And there won't be any talk about him moving back in again until we get a clean accounting of what the hell happened to Pete's money."

She was horrified to think anybody would have stolen from Pete, but to think it might have been his own brother, that made it so much worse. "Did he really steal money from him?"

"Ross has another two and a half hours to make good on the amount that's supposed to be there," he said. "And believe me, Pete is checking bank accounts, and so are the accountants. Pete got a lump sum after he got back, for lost wages and to help with medical adjustments. And every damn penny of that had better be there," he said coolly. "Or none of the law around this area will do anything to help Ross. I'll make sure he's slammed into some jail a long way away without any support system for a hell of a long time."

"As long as you leave him alive, and you don't break any bones doing it," Jessie said, his tone hard, "I won't argue."

"I might break a bone or two," Pierce said with a fat smile. "But, of course, that's only if he struggles. If he's a good boy and behaves himself, then"—Pierce shrugged—"no need to force him to do anything, is there?"

The two men exchanged knowing looks.

Just then Ross came back out with a duffel bag and another bag. "The rest of my stuff is still here," he said. "I can't take it all right now."

"That's fine. I'll have a talk with Pete and get an inventory of what belongs here and what you say is yours." He looked at the two bags. "Make sure it's just your shit in there because I'll come back after you if anything from the house is missing."

Ross shot him a look full of hatred. "It's mine." He threw the bags in the back of the pickup and walked to where Jed was.

The two men talked, glanced at Pierce, the conversation continued, then they both got into their vehicles and pulled out.

Jessie and the men with him walked up to the veranda, Jessie saying, "You just made yourself a couple enemies."

Hedi laughed. "And yet, it's you, Dad, who always said you could judge a man by the enemies he makes."

Jessie nodded. "I did, indeed. But these are especially ugly ones. They'll torch this place before they'll let you have it."

Pierce narrowed his gaze as he studied the men driving away. "In that case somebody might want to make sure Jed's wife and kids go someplace for a few days until we get this sorted out," he said, "because ugly is what ugly does."

Hedi wasn't sure what the hell that meant, but she understood the meaning. "You can't get those kids caught up in this," she warned. "They're already having a hell of a time."

"He's right though," her father said. "Things will have to get worse before they get any better."

She frowned, then turned to face Pierce again. "I talked to Jed's wife. She said there are signs of a dog out in the back here. She doesn't know if it's the same one or not. It's circling away from Jed's place, but Pete's place is also Salem's last-known source of food, outside of anything it can hunt."

Pierce smiled. "Now that's the best news I've heard all day."

"How can that be?" she said. "That dog has gone half wild."

"But it always was half wild," he said. "That's what makes them the best War Dogs. If we could get our hands on her, I can help her."

"Do you really think you can?"

He nodded. "It's a good thing I did move in here today," he said. "I'll work hard to get Salem back in line, see if we can get her rehabilitated in time for Pete to come home. That's where they both belong—with each other."

Jessie nodded. "I can swing a hammer, maybe not as good as you can, but I can certainly do a decent job." He looked at the other couple guys, and they all nodded. "If there's anything we can do to help get Pete's house ready, you just let us know."

Pierce smiled.

Hedi laughed. "Thanks, Dad."

He looked at her and smiled. "I wish you had a different job. I don't know where the sheriff will fall on this issue, but it'll get bad."

"I know." Her voice was serious and sad. "It's shitty, but it's the way it'll be."

"Maybe you should head back into town then," Pierce said.

"Why, so I don't get hurt?" she challenged. "I'm the deputy. Remember that."

"Then I hope you're carrying," he said, "because you can bet Jed's gone home to get some firepower."

She looked at him, then nodded. "You're right. He probably has. But Jed is also not the kind of guy who would blast you in the face. He'll come up behind you, shoot you in the back."

"Nice community you have here." Pierce crossed his arms over his chest again. "I might have to call in some reinforcements of my own."

Jessie nodded. "If you got them, call them fast."

"I'll move my vehicle out of sight," she said. "Just in case."

"Good idea," Jessie said.

Hedi drove her car around to the side and parked it. She hopped out and walked up to the front of the house and stepped in without warning. Pierce turned around, surprised, and took note. "You move softly."

"I'm a cop," she said.

He nodded. "Why are you here now?"

"Because you'll need help," she said. "It could get very ugly."

"It could," he said, hesitating.

She stared at him. "Unless you've got a problem with a female helping."

"I don't have a problem with a female helping," he said with a grin. "Don't suppose you can swing a hammer too, can you?"

She could feel the tension ease in her back. "I can swing a hammer pretty decently. I helped my father do enough renos and fixing up fence posts and barn repairs," she said.

"Good enough for me." Pierce motioned at the kitchen. "I'm sorting out what's here and what's been done to the place since Pete was here." Just then his phone rang. It was Pete again. "Hey, Pete. Yeah, Hedi is here."

Through the phone she could hear Pete call out, "Hey, Hedi. Hi."

She grinned, leaned forward and said, "Hey, Pete. Pierce has kicked the metaphorical shit out of your brother and moved him off your property, and now you got this big mausoleum of a house waiting for you to get your sorry ass back home again."

Pete gave a big laugh.

She grinned, looked at Pierce and smiled. "If there's one thing Pete does like, it's life."

"Pete used to like life," Pete said, still shouting into the phone. "And he's starting to like life again."

"You hit a rough spot," Pierce said, "and all of a sudden that rough spot became too much to handle. You have to get through it first. Then life is different on the other side."

"Now I'm starting to believe," he said. "You will never guess, but I got a phone call from a prosthetic designer who says she thinks she can help me out." He spoke with amazement. "I told her that I had to sort out my money first, and she agreed, said she needed permission to get my medical records to see what she could do. Of course I gave her my permission, like *Holy shit, yes.* If I could actually *walk*, as in walk on my own two legs, that would be huge."

Pierce chuckled. "That's Kat. And she's dynamite. She's also an amputee herself, so, if she says she can do something for you, she can do something for you."

"Holy shit. I'm so damn grateful. I feel like everything has flipped around now."

"But that doesn't mean you're over the hump yet," Pierce warned. "You take good care of yourself. I'll hang up and see if I can find some bloody coffee in this place. Then I'll work out some modifications for the house, and we'll sit down and talk money, once we sort out the bank account, what you have left."

"Okay, will do," Pete said, his voice slowing, hesitating. "I know this shit is expensive, so it needs to be just, you know, basics to begin with."

Pete said goodbye, and Pierce shut off the call. "Do you have any idea where the coffee might be in here?"

He turned around to see Hedi already opening cupboards. She smiled at him. "Who knows?" She pulled out an almost empty bag of coffee. "It's enough for one pot." She filled the coffeemaker and had a pot brewing quickly. She turned around, took one look at him, studying him for a long moment. "Why are you doing this?"

He'd been looking at his phone, checking for messages. At her words, he stopped and looked up at her. His gaze was open and serious. "I came to rescue a dog. But War Dogs are War Dogs, both man and animal. I've been there, done that, and, if I can give a helping hand to another veteran, I'm all in. Pete's got a bum deal here. I'm not sure what the hell is going on with Jed and Ross, and whoever else is hanging around that same crowd, but they're all bad news."

"Oh, I know they're bad news," she said quietly. "But, like I said before—you've stepped into the middle of a hornet's nest, and you've got it all stirred up."

"Good," he said. "Time to swat those little buggers." He looked out the window, his gaze caught on something.

"What do you see?"

"The shepherd is hanging around the house," he said.

She looked but couldn't see what was bothering him.

"I don't want to put food out. She needs to know she can come in and get food."

"Any time she's gotten close to men lately," Hedi said seriously, "she's gotten hurt. Maybe you should give a little to break the ice."

"I might have to," he said, pondering the issue. He got up to poke through the fridge and freezer. "If there was at least a bone or something, I could give it to her. Even dog food would help."

"There should have been some. Ross said he had an intruder who stole everything, but I figure Jed just came and took it all," Hedi said. "Let me help you look. They might have missed something."

Together they went through the cabinets. Triumphantly Hedi found the remnants of an old bag in the back corner. "I bet he forgot about this one. There's only four, maybe six cups, but it'll give the dog something to start with." She handed Pierce the bag and watched as he dumped it all into a large bowl and walked out back.

He judged the distance between him and where he'd seen the dog; then he put down several piles, one farther away, another closer, and then another one closer yet. The last one he left in the bowl itself. Then he walked back inside and poured a cup of coffee.

"What makes you think she'll come in?"

"She's hungry," he said. "She's also apparently scared and worried about getting caught. If she's been that badly abused, then she'll stay away from all men. But this is also home to her and probably has some good memories."

"Yes," she said, nodding. "How quickly can Pete get back here?"

"I'm not sure," he said, taking a sip of his coffee. "But, once we get him home, if we haven't got any modifications done, we'll find a way to make some quick and fast changes for him. The kitchen is a problem. It's open enough, but the area to sit, it's pretty small, pretty crowded."

She walked to the wall behind the island where the dining room table sat. "If this wall isn't structural, why not take it out?"

He nodded, looking up at the way the joists and the ceiling met with the walls. "I don't think it is structural." He looked from the wall to the countertop that extended far out. "That would probably give him enough access. He can work at the counters, but this outside piece here ... Yeah, you're right. That might be the best answer." He looked at it for a long moment. "It's just drywall. I could probably pop that off in no time, see just what the framing is like. If it's simple, I could take it down."

"It'll be the electrical threading through the walls that would cause trouble," she said.

"Not really," he said. "I can do almost all house wiring. I just can't do high-voltage stuff."

She looked at him in surprise. "It sounds like you're a pretty handy guy to have around."

He shrugged. "You learn to do an awful lot when you're flipping houses. I can put in sinks and do basic plumbing too, but, if you want fancy stuff, I don't know. I might need some help."

"Do you think you can modify the bathroom?"

He frowned at her. "I can. I'm just not sure I could make it look decorator pretty. He needs to have access to the toilet with handicap bars, and he needs a wheelchair-accessible sink and shower stall. Would a shower chair work? I'll have to do some research on that. Maybe talk to these friends of mine."

"Are they amputees too?"

He grinned. "Yes. Eight former SEALs began Titanium Corp, and all are missing at least an arm or a leg or both," he said, roaming the kitchen with an eye toward renovations. "Lots of back injuries too. Steel plates, all kinds of extras they weren't born with."

"What about you?" she asked. "Are you missing body parts?"

"Sure I am," he said. "Lots of tissue, muscle, a chunk of liver, gallbladder, one kidney, and"—he kicked out his leg—"I'm missing the lower leg."

"So you really do understand what Pete's going

through."

"I do," he said. "And I know, if he's over the hump, he'll be okay now. But we have to do everything we can to make it possible for him to come home."

"He's missing both legs below the knees I believe, or is one above?"

"He's missing both lower legs," Pierce said. "Lots of guys without both legs can still walk."

"So you're trying to make room for a wheelchair as a contingency while he gets better or when he's too tired or if he has an injury and needs to be in the wheelchair. But, other than that, he should be capable of walking with prosthetics?"

"Potentially down the road. It takes time for the body to heal before attaching the new limbs. Plus he's got some back injuries, so we have to strengthen that up. Let's just say he has a lot of work ahead of him."

"But it's doable?"

He looked at her in surprise. "It's absolutely doable. That's why I'm here, to help make it happen as much as we can."

"But that's not what you came for."

"No, it isn't." He looked out the window for Salem, turned and added, "That seems to bug you. Yes, I came for the dog, but then I found out what was happening at Pete's place. It's really no contest. The two dovetail together. If Pete can come home, the dog gets a home again, and then somebody just needs to keep an eye on Pete to make sure he doesn't have any setbacks and that the dog is still okay."

She laughed. "I can't tell if you care more about Pete or the dog."

"Doesn't matter," Pierce said. "They both need help,

and we've got to get both back home. In the meantime, I've apparently stirred up some angry people."

"That you have," she said.

"Is that why you're here?" he asked. "You don't think I can handle this on my own?"

"I think it's quite possible my dad's right, and they'll likely burn this place to the ground before they let you have it."

He studied her face for a long moment. "And nobody will do anything to stop them?"

"You saw the sheriff. He just backs away anytime there's a fight."

"What happens when the people are fed up with the sheriff? How do you get rid of him?"

"We have to go above him."

"What if he quits?" Pierce's voice was almost a challenge.

"Then somebody has a temporary promotion until a new election."

"Interesting," Pierce said. "I don't do politics. I'm too much of a person who likes to get things done, and screw it if people are happy or unhappy with it."

"Are you still registered at the hotel?" she asked, leaning against the counter, sipping her coffee.

He refilled his cup and faced her. "No. I checked out this morning."

"So you had already planned to move in today?"

"I was happy to have his brother stay, particularly if I thought he would give us a hand with the reno. But I don't want any more deadbeats bringing Pete down."

She nodded. "So did you bring groceries?"

"Not yet," he said cheerfully. "I can make a trip to town."

"You probably don't want to leave right now," she said. "Ross is likely to have somebody keeping a lookout to see if you do. And, once you're gone, he'll be back with company. You'll find it much harder to get back in."

"Right. Good point," he said. "I think I've got a few protein bars in the truck, and that might have to do, if there isn't anything around here." He opened the fridge and snorted. "If I'm staying here, I need to get some food. Ross obviously doesn't care about actual nutrition."

"Since it seems I'm coming back this evening, why don't I pick up some basics?"

He turned and looked at her. "Why are you coming back?"

"Same reason I'm here now," she said. "I don't like the idea of you being alone with that gang. They'll lose their tempers with you."

"Oh." He grinned. "It sounds good to me. I'm so glad you're worried about me, sweetie."

She narrowed her gaze at him. "The name is Hedi. Don't call me sweetie."

"Okay. I won't, sweetheart. Hedi's kind of a slang nickname anyway, isn't it?"

She fisted her hands on her hips and glared at him.

He chuckled, opening a cabinet, finding cereal. "Let's do a quick list. Don't know exactly what's available, but we could use some milk for this cereal, if nothing else. Some eggs, bread, and bacon for breakfast." He rummaged through some of the other cupboards. "There's really nothing here. Salad fixings, pasta, maybe a pack or two of hamburger, some buns, that type of thing. Can you handle that?"

"I can handle that," she said, "as long as you don't care about the quality and are happy with the choices I make."

"It's food," he said. "I'll be happy." He pulled his wallet from his back pocket, pulled out two hundred dollars and handed it to her. "Groceries," he said.

She looked at the money in surprise. "That's a lot of grocery money."

"I've got to eat, and I've got to work," he said. "Just make sure you pick up some dog food and not too cheap of a brand. Salem'll need real food. Thinking of which, better make that several packages of ground beef. I could always get her to eat meat too."

Hedi walked out to her car. The sun was beginning to set. "I'll be at least an hour, probably twice that."

"Not a problem," he said. "I'll cook dinner for you when you get in, depending on how late it is."

"I'm likely to pick up dinner instead."

"If there's any money left, go for it," he said. "I'll start working on ramps. That's probably the easiest thing to begin with. I saw a lot of wood in the barn, and I can certainly get something started while you're out and about."

She nodded. "You take care." And she headed back into town.

SUCH AN INTERESTING woman. And a novelty to have somebody pitch in and help. He hated the idea of her getting caught up in this mess though. Still, just the thought of her made him smile. He did have a lot of good friends, and he was concerned about giving a heads-up to Badger. Thinking of that, he stopped what he was doing, pulled out his phone and updated him.

Badger's response was immediate. "Do you want some

backup?"

"The deputy is coming back, but I'm not exactly sure when she'll make it. It's a pretty strange scenario," he admitted. "I think Jessie, her father, who's the former sheriff, would be here in a pinch, but it's not the same as having men of your own."

"Let me talk to Pete and see if anybody in town can help you out."

"Okay. He's the one who contacted Hedi's dad, the ex-sheriff. And we need to figure out what to do about the current sheriff."

"Yeah, that's a bad one," Badger said. "I'll get back to you on that." And he hung up.

Pierce put the phone on the table and something caught his eyes. He looked up to see a massive black shepherd wolfing down the bit of dog food he'd put at the farthest point out. Pierce walked to the open doorway and stepped out on the porch. She froze and stared at him. "It's all right, Salem. I know you've had a pretty shitty time, but we're getting you back here, and Pete's coming home too."

Her ears twitched, but that was all. She kept eating, her eyes focused on him. If he took one step toward her, he knew she'd bolt. He kept his voice low and steady, just talking to her, leaning against the porch railing. "Make sure you eat up. You'll need it. I've got more food coming, but it'll be a few hours yet."

She finished the pile in front of her and raised her head, still studying him, her muscles tense, ready. She glanced to the side, as if hearing a sound, then hunkered down a little lower, but her gaze never left that area.

"Is something there? Wouldn't be at all surprised. Some two-legged wolves are in this part of the country," he said.

"They might be foolish enough to attack."

Then she seemed to relax at the constant voice talking to her. She moved a step closer.

"You can do it," he said. "Come on to the next pile. You need it. That's nowhere near enough food for you yet."

She took a few more steps in. Her nose had already caught the scent of the next pile. Nervously she crept forward enough so that she could devour the second pile.

"Come on. Eat it up," he said in an encouraging tone.

She was big. Her coat was shaggy and matted. She limped, and blood was on her flank but there didn't appear to be an open wound. She moved slowly, and she was injured, but she wasn't that badly physically hurt. However, the look in her eyes was one of betrayal, one that said she didn't trust anybody anymore, and that broke his heart.

He took two slow steps down the porch, stopped and sat. She froze, her mouth full of food, but not chewing as she watched him. He stayed in place and just kept talking to her. Finally she lowered her head and ate the rest of the food.

"So what did you do? Just got loose from the police yard? How did they catch you again? Probably with food and that's why you're so nervous." He looked around the area. There should have been fences around the homestead itself. It was a nice property, and, with a little bit of care, it could be quite a nice place, depending on how much land he had here. Pete could possibly have crops that could either help him out grocery-wise or be something he could sell and make a little money.

Pierce sat here quietly, content while the dog ate. When the third pile was gone, she looked at him and backed up slightly. The bowl was just a little too close to Pierce.

"It'll be here for you. You've had three piles. That'll take the worst of the hunger off."

She continued to back up. When something crackled in the bush beside him, she spun and raced off. He was happy to see her movements were clean and powerful. She held her back leg too low to the ground for a clean run, but then she was injured. He couldn't really tell how or how badly, but at least she'd been fed.

He walked to the side of the house where he'd heard crackling in a bush. He wasn't sure what was out here, if it was another dog or a wild animal or something he was quite prepared to beat into the ground. He did a quick search but saw nothing.

As he was about to walk away, he heard a meow. He turned to see a ragtag cat walking toward him. It didn't look underfed, but it didn't look terribly healthy either. He stopped and bent down. "Hey, kitty. What are you doing here?"

"*Meow, meow.*" The cat sauntered closer. It looked like a tomcat, part of an ear torn, patch of fur missing.

He didn't know if he'd been fighting other cats or taking down prey a little too big for him. Pierce reached out a hand, scooped it up, not surprised when the cat allowed him to pick him up. With the cat in his arms, he walked to the barn. "There should be a ton of food for you in here. Barns always have mice." He scratched the guy behind the ear, listening to the great big guttural engine kick in, and smiled. "You're probably Pete's too, aren't you?"

In the barn he put the cat on a bale of hay, then stopped and stared, finally struck by what he saw before him. "Pete, why do you have hay? I don't see any horses or cows." But there was hay, a good forty, maybe sixty bales of it. He frowned, hoping Ross hadn't sold off livestock that Pete had owned.

Pierce turned to the wood supply. Found at least six good solid sheets of plywood. A full sheet would be too broad, but he took out his tape measure and marked off what he needed. What he also needed was some solid tools.

He headed into the open workshop and found a circular saw and a few power tools. He grinned when he saw those. "Thought I would have to do this the old-fashioned way."

"And just what's the old-fashioned way?"

He turned to see Ross standing stiffly in the doorway. Pierce looked at him. "By hand," he said.

"This is by hand," Ross said in exasperation as he pointed at the tools. "Who the hell even knows how to operate this old shit?"

"It's not that old," Pierce said. "I imagine almost all of it is in good working condition."

"Maybe, but it's old," Ross said in disgust.

"What's with the hay? What are you doing back here?" Pierce asked as he continued to mark and measure the board in front of him.

"I left some stuff here, remember?" Ross's tone was only half derisive. He knew he'd get his face kicked in if he didn't show enough respect. "Pete used to board some city horses here. I sent them home. Way too much work to look after."

"Sorted your money issue yet?" Pierce asked thinking how foolish he was to wipe out a source of income. Then anything that required effort appeared to be too much for Ross.

"I still got an hour," he said.

"Is that all? I hadn't realized the time had gone by so fast. I figured you were already out of time."

"You said eight," Ross said in alarm.

Pierce slowly straightened and looked at him. "I said four."

"No, you said four hours, and it's only seven now."

"The question is whether you've done the job, or will I find out you've stolen your brother's money? And, of course, that'll definitely get your ass kicked across the property."

"How would you know?" Ross asked with a laugh.

"Because Pete's got the accountants and the bookkeepers and the police on his end tracking his account."

The color drained from Ross's face. "Pete wouldn't do that to me."

"Pete has to start looking after Pete," Pierce said. "And other people should be looking after Pete, not him looking after you. You're able-bodied and not working. You should be out there pulling in a decent wage, doing something with your own life, not trying to take what's your brother's."

"Don't be so sanctimonious and righteous," Ross said. "I've been living here and kept people like Jed off the place."

"That may be," he said, "but you're also making deals with Jed too, and Jed's bad news in his own right."

"He is that," Ross said. "He's gotten a lot worse these last six months."

"What's that all about?"

Ross just shrugged. "I don't know. Something about his wife wanting a divorce."

"Of course she wants a divorce," Pierce said with a laugh of his own. "Why the hell would she want to stay and get her ass kicked every day? Watch her kids be terrorized?"

"He won't let her go," Ross said starkly.

"Are you going to help him?" Pierce asked. "You don't seem to have too much in the way of ethics or honor."

"That's not fair," Ross muttered. "I didn't see I was doing nothing wrong."

"The trouble is, when you take a half step across the line, it's pretty easy to take another half step, and, before you know it," Pierce said, "you've taken so many steps you can't even see the line anymore. At that point, in your twisted mind, you're already thinking it's all yours. And you're blowing it on booze and forgetting even about food."

"I've had a pretty rough couple months myself," he said. "So I took a few dollars. That's not a big deal. Pete would never begrudge me that."

"Well, just think, it's not Pete's deal anymore," Pierce said. "It's mine. And I'll make sure Pete gets what's his. Whether you like it or not."

CHAPTER 7

HEDI CASHED OUT at the grocery store and took her loaded bags to her deputy's car. She would go home and change vehicles. She could already feel the tension in the air. Weird discussions behind her back. People looking at her sideways but not really talking to her.

She ignored everybody and kept walking to the car. "Small-town news travels fast," she muttered under her breath.

When she got home, she planned to park around back to make sure she wasn't seen. She had one handgun with her, and she wondered about picking up more from her dad's. And hated that she was even thinking along those lines.

Just then she got a phone call. She hit Talk. "Hey, Dad. How you doing?"

"I'm doing okay, but I'm a little worried about that Pierce guy out there. I really admire what he's doing for Pete, but he might have bitten off more than he can chew. Have you got an update?"

"I just bought groceries, so he didn't have to leave the place, in case Ross came back and didn't want to give up possession again."

"Good idea," he said thoughtfully. "I can't say I'm feeling too good about this."

"I know," she said, "but I think Pierce's heart is in the

right place. I just don't know if he understands how bad Jed has gotten."

"I'm not sure I understand either. Can you explain it to me?"

She told him about Jed attacking her in his house and shoving her with his rifle and threatening her. "I guess you didn't read the emails I cc'd you on, did you?"

"No, I'm sorry. I've been avoiding the computer. As you know it's not my preferred method of communication. But this…" Her father swore up and down a blue streak. "And that damn sheriff didn't do anything?"

"Nope. He's pretty cozy with Jed, and, as long as Jed stays on this side of the law, he doesn't care."

"But that was not on *this side of the law*," her father snapped. "What has this come to?"

"Hate to say it, Dad, but, when you got in that accident, all hell went to a shithole."

"I can see that," he grumbled. "I'm not sure I could pick up the reins and be sheriff again though. I kind of like retirement. I'll talk to Fort Collins, see what our next step is in ousting our current sheriff."

"You like retirement and no need to go back. But please find out how to get rid of our sheriff. He'll get someone killed with his negligence," she admitted as she moved the last of the groceries over and locked up her deputy vehicle. "What you don't like is sitting on the sidelines. So feel free to fix this. If anyone can, it's you."

"I hear you there. Do you think somebody needs to come to the house and stand watch tonight?"

"I'm heading there now myself," she said. "The sheriff won't call it on duty, but I sure as hell am. Pierce might have taken on more than he can chew. I don't know him well enough. It's not just Jed. You know he's got the Billy boys in the back, and, if he gets them all riled up, they'll shoot that place down, and they'll torch it with him in it."

"You in it too, you mean," her father said in alarm. "Maybe I'll come over myself."

"I won't say no," she said. "But we could be jumping the gun here. It wouldn't be a bad idea to have a watch on what Jed is up to, but I don't know. Those kids and his wife, she was supposed to leave. I called her at work today, and she promised me that she would, but I just don't know. I don't have a good feeling about any of this."

"Neither do I." Her father's voice suddenly sounded brisk. "You go on over. I'll call the boys and see what we come up with." And just like that he hung up.

She frowned, staring at her phone. "But I don't need to be looking after you too, Dad. You're not the law anymore," she said slowly.

She walked back into the house and grabbed an overnight bag and stuffed it in the car. She didn't know what the hell would happen, but she wanted to be prepared. She also grabbed one of her big thick flannel shirts in case it got really cold out tonight. She didn't know how much she would be in the house or outside, so she chose her black one, just to blend in the background. She wasn't the hunter the others were, but she was no slouch when it came to hiding her tracks and staying out of sight.

The last thing she did was put out some cat food and fed her dog. She had a small Maltese that was aging and wouldn't appreciate being alone tonight, but she couldn't take him into a gunfight. He was all about curling up on her pillow and being cuddled. He didn't like loud noises or aggressive moves. He'd be fine if it was a normal visit, but tonight could get ugly.

She arranged his blanket on the couch for him and walked away, locking up behind her.

In her own vehicle, she drove toward Pete's place. The air had an electric feel to it, the atmosphere felt off, wrong in so many ways.

Following her instincts, she drove into the barn and parked. There was an old blanket, kind of a car cover there. She threw it over her car as soon as she had the groceries out. It took her two trips to get the groceries to the house, but, with everything stacked on the front veranda, she knocked on the door and then pushed it open.

A light was on in the living room, but everything else appeared quiet. Frowning, she grabbed her grocery bags and carried everything into the kitchen, setting it all on the table. Outside she could see Pierce sitting on the steps only ten feet away from Salem. Her ears were back, and her lip was curled, but she was the one approaching him.

Standing still, she watched as man and dog slowly tried to work out their differences. She could see the bowl was a good twenty feet away, and it appeared emptied and flipped over. Pierce had something in his hand, which he held out for her. Salem wanted it badly but didn't come any closer. Pierce took off a piece and threw it in front of her. It didn't land on the ground because she snatched it out of the air and gobbled it down, then turned to look at him again expectantly. But she wasn't coming any closer.

Hedi smiled as she studied Salem's large frame. She was a good fifty pounds over the normal weight of a shepherd, so some other breed was mixed in there. Her feet were huge, and her jaw was massive. Hedi had only ever seen Salem more aggressive than calm. She wondered what she was like around Pete.

Hedi walked to the open doorway as she watched Pierce toss another piece toward Salem, and she snatched it up and waited. He spoke to Hedi, his voice at the same low pitch. "Step on the porch."

Obediently she did so and quietly called out, "Hi, Salem."

Salem's ears twitched, and her gaze darted toward her, then back to Pierce again.

"Can I come closer?" Hedi asked.

"Slowly walk toward me," he said quietly.

She did as she was told. "She doesn't see me as a threat, does she?"

"Are women known to have beaten her?"

"I don't think so," she said. "I've only ever fed her and given her water."

"Which is why she's not afraid of you. She'll be cautious, just in case you are like the men she's met, but you're not one of the main threats. I am."

"It's good instincts on her part then, isn't it?" she said, a note of humor in her voice. "I'm surprised she's this close to you."

"I'm not. I've been at it since you left," he said. "I hope you brought home some food though, because I'm starved."

"I did, indeed. But I'm not cooking it," she warned. "I might have been the delivery person, but I sure as hell am not a cook."

"Did you bring fast food too?"

"I did, in the sense that I brought subs."

"Oh, yum," he said, standing up slowly, still tossing food toward the hungry dog. "Salem, sweetie, I'll go in and get some food myself." He took two steps back, and Salem's butt hit the ground. She looked up at him, her ears straight up.

"It's almost as if she understands you," Hedi said.

"She does," Pierce said quietly. "I've been working on a few of the commands she would know from Pete's training. I gave her the Sit command just now with a hand signal, and she did it without argument. So we've come a long way." He looked around. "If there was a dog bed still around, it should be something for her use on the deck. Even though she'll probably be a while getting back into the house, it would be good to know she feels like this is home again."

"I think I saw something in the barn," she said. "Give me a moment."

She took off slowly at first, so as not to spook Salem, and headed toward the barn, where she took the big car cover. It might be more of a horse blanket, but it would do the job. It was large, at least a four foot by three foot. Carrying it with great difficulty out of the barn and to the deck, she place it close to the steps. "Maybe this'll do."

He looked at it and nodded approvingly. "It probably was a horse blanket, but it's thick, so I'm not sure. As long as she thinks maybe it's for her, it'll be fine." He motioned for Hedi to back up into the kitchen, then he turned deliberately and walked inside, leaving the door open. "Now we'll see what she does."

He took one look at the subs on the counter and grinned. She smiled to see such joy on his face. It was a good thing she brought two twelve-inch subs since she was hungry herself. She unwrapped the first one and cut it in four pieces. The subs were made from whole French bread loaves.

He reached for the quarter portion closest to him and then stopped and looked at her. "Do you want me to have an end piece instead?"

"We each get an end piece," she explained, "but I'm starting with a center piece." She flashed him a grin and walked to the counter. "Damn. I did buy coffee, just didn't start any. I guess we can put some on afterward." She sat at the small rickety table and frowned. "I don't think this was Pete's table. He had a big oak one from his granddad."

"It's possible," Pierce said. "I'm not sure what Ross might have sold."

Just then she heard noises upstairs. "What's that?" she cried out in a harsh whisper.

"Ross," he said. "He came to get the rest of his stuff. This is his second trip."

"How do you know it's his stuff though?" she asked.

"Because I'm taking pictures of it and checking with Pete. If it's just personal shit, I don't think Pete cares. He was trying to take some of the electronics, and Pete says those are his. We're also having an argument about how much money he owes Pete. From the looks of it, he needs to replace close to thirty thousand dollars that he stole."

"I didn't steal it," Ross snapped from the doorway, "and I ain't paying it back." He turned and looked at her. "Hey, I mean, really I didn't steal it." His voice turned into a whine. "Pete's got no reason to say that."

"Thirty thousand dollars?" she said. "What did you do with all that money? Pete needs that to fix up the house."

Ross raise both hands, palms exposed, in obvious frustration. "Well, I didn't know he was coming back, did I?"

"That's hardly any reason to steal from your brother." She turned to look at Pierce. "Pete doesn't have much money."

"Oh, he's got money, his pension if nothing else," Pierce said. "We'll have to go through the courts, obviously, to get the money back though."

"I don't have the money," Ross said. "I told you that."

Pierce turned and looked at him, pinning him in place. "A lien has been slapped on your account," he said. "I got confirmation of that twenty minutes ago. You won't be getting any of that money out of that account until an agreement is made."

"You can't do that," he blubbered. "I don't have any money for gas."

"Isn't that just too damn bad," Pierce said, standing, towering above him. "Isn't it too damn bad you stole so much money from your brother? According to the lien, over sixty thousand dollars is in that account. And I want to know where it came from. Like, where is Pete's antique dining room table?"

Ross shook his head. "No. You can't touch that money. That's *my* money."

"I know of at least thirty thousand you took from Pete. But, for all I know, it's a lot more than that, and that's why we'll do a full investigation before you get access again."

"You can't do that."

"Too damn bad, too late. A lawsuit has been filed. A lien has been slapped. Now you should get a lawyer, and you can fight it out."

"How am I supposed to pay for a lawyer," he cried out, "if I can't get my money?"

"Stealing it from your brother doesn't make it *your* money. I guess you have a problem then, don't you?"

Hedi stepped forward and said, "Ross, did you really steal that kind of money from Pete?" She knew assholes were in this world, but to steal from your disabled brother? ... That was pretty low.

He looked at her sadly. "I didn't think Pete would need it. It seems like the government paid for everything for him, so what did he need the money for? I needed it."

"What did you need it for?" she asked, puzzled. "You've been living in Pete's house free and clear, Pete's paying the bills, the taxes, according to what Pierce has said. So what did you need the money for?

"Because I don't want to stay here," he cried out. "And, even if I can't sell Pete's place, and if I want to get the hell out of here, I have to have cash."

"When were you thinking of selling Pete's place?" she asked. "Did you ask him about that?"

"Yeah, but he won't sell." Ross snorted. "Look at this place. It's falling down. I won't get much for it anyway. As much as it's nice to have free room and board, I do have to think about my own future."

"Where did you get all the money from then?" Pierce asked.

"It's mine," Ross snapped. "I was working, you know? Right up until I lost my job a few months back. I saved it."

"You saved it because you were living at Pete's place," Pierce said.

"And did you sell a bunch of stuff from Pete's home?" Hedi said, looking back at the kitchen table. "He had that wonderful antique table from your granddad. That was Pete's. Where is it?" She caught a glimpse of something in the back of Ross's eyes. She stared at him. "Did you really strip his house of everything of value and sell it?"

"Just a few things," he said. "He was my granddad too."

"But according to Pete," she said, "you got cash, and he wanted the heirlooms."

"I ran through the cash pretty damn fast. It wasn't much

anyway. Maybe five grand."

"Likely two to three times that. Pete should know. That sixty grand came from somewhere. Thirty of it came from Pete's pension account. So you sure as hell don't get to keep any of that," she said, a cool note entering her voice. "If we find any of the rest of it is Pete's inheritance from his granddad …" She let her words hang as she looked at Pierce to see him already sending a message on his phone. She figured it was probably to Pete, who likely would face even more shocks. She spun to look at Ross. "Is the rest of that money from stripping out the house and selling everything you could? Ignoring that the stuff really mattered to Pete because it was the stuff that would bring in the most money?"

"It's just garbage," Ross said, throwing up his hands. "Who gives a shit about a table and chairs anyway?"

"Pete did," Pierce said, holding up his phone. "That's a piece he loved, and apparently he's more than pissed at you. And he wants to know how much and where you sold that, so he can go buy it back."

"There's no way. It's already been sold," he said. "I made a deal with a guy in town."

"Which guy?" Hedi said, crossing her arms and staring at him with loathing. She turned to look at Pierce. "Any way to check if he's got other bank accounts too? Seems like one might be too simple for him."

Ross just shook his head. "Jesus Christ. You'll make sure I have nothing left by the time you're done," he snapped.

"You mean, like your brother?" she asked.

"But the government will take care of him until he dies," Ross roared. "Don't you guys see how unfair that is? He doesn't have to worry about nothing. He gets his medical coverage. He gets enough money every month to pay for all his needs. He never has to work again."

"It's not free," Pierce said. "He was over there fighting for his country while you were sitting here drinking beer. Now he's done his time and paid the price with heavy injuries, and you're sitting here, in *his* house, like a jealous little schoolboy, wanting what he had without having to go through the work and pain he went through."

"Whatever," Ross said as he looked at the groceries behind them. "Since you've locked up all my money"—his was voice full of sarcasm—"any chance I can have a bit of that sandwich? I haven't eaten all day."

Hedi picked up the other quarter of her half and handed it to him. "I want to make sure you don't take anything else from this place. Pierce said he will go through this next load of yours just as well as he did the others."

Ross glared at her. "It's my place too, you know?"

"No, it's not," Pierce said cheerfully. "The deed is in Pete's name. You may have tried to get him to sell, but it's his and his alone. And it's also paid for. So, if nothing else, Pete has a place to live for the rest of his life."

"Which is more than I have," Ross said bitterly.

"You *could* have," Hedi said. "You could have made arrangements to put a mobile home here or to build a small house or to even share this with him. But instead all you've done is take from him. Good riddance to you when you walk out that door."

Ross shook his head, shoving the sandwich in his mouth, bite after bite after bite. And, when it was finally gone, he gave a heavy sigh. "At least I've got a full stomach." He walked to the front door where his duffel bag was. "I don't think you guys realize what you've brought down on your heads."

"Why is that?" Pierce said. "What did you have to offer these guys so that they'll be pissed off that Pete's back at home?"

"It's not about Pete," he said. "Well, it is, but not really. I let them have access to the property for their moonshine, and, for that, they turn a blind eye when I move stuff out." He grinned and shook his head again. "Jed doesn't need an excuse. He's just got blood in his eyes, and, for any reason, it's an outlet for that anger of his," Ross added. "I kind of wish Vicky would get the hell away from him. She doesn't deserve it."

"What about the Billy boys?" Hedi said. "They're Jed's buddies too."

"Oh, yeah, they are, and you better watch yourselves. They're twins, and, when Jed says, *Jump*, they ask, *How high?* They'll be coming here tonight. Don't you worry. Why the hell do you think I'm getting all my shit out of here? I want out before this place goes up in smoke." He walked to the front door.

Pierce grabbed the duffel bag, took it to the couch where he dropped it, opening it up. He removed all the electronics that had been stacked up. "No way you're taking Pete's laptop or tablet. And this is a monitor. Stuffing it in here is hardly a good way to treat it. We'll be lucky if you didn't damage it. And where the hell is the desktop?"

"I don't think it works anymore," he said resentfully. "I need a laptop too, you know? I gotta find work now. How the hell am I supposed to do that?"

"You can try your phone," she said in a conversational tone. "Which is probably Pete's, considering it's a brand-new iPhone."

Ross shoved the phone in his pocket. "It's mine," he snapped. "You can't take that from me too."

"Guess that's more to ask Pete about, isn't it?" Pierce stepped off to the side, lifted his phone to his head and called Pete again.

Hedi smiled at Ross, who sagged on the couch. "You really have done it to yourself, haven't you? Not only is everybody here pissed at you, but everybody in town, once they hear what you did to your own brother, will be too." She shook her head.

There was a loud sound outside. Ross straightened up and said, "Shit, shit, shit. I've got to go." He pulled the rest of his stuff into the duffel bag and closed it up, racing to the front door. As he approached it, a bullet went right through the solid wood, just missing him. He hit the ground, crying out, "Shit! Look what you've done."

"Oh, yeah, I'm watching all right," Hedi said from behind the window. Sure enough, there was Jed and the Billy boys. "You didn't get out fast enough. You were too greedy. Now you're here. You know they'll make you take a side, and, if it isn't their side, they'll put a bullet in your head." The trouble was, she knew she was right. That was exactly what they would do. She pulled out her phone and sent her dad a text message. **You better come, and bring some firepower. Jed and the Billy boys are here, and they're on a rampage.**

PIERCE BARELY MANAGED to get connected to Pete when the bullet came through the door. From the corner of the living room, he stared at the three men outside.

Pete called out, "What am I hearing?"

"Someone just shot through your door," Pierce said, "barely missed your brother. He was trying to run out with another duffel bag full of electronics, like your laptop and your monitor."

Pete started swearing again. "That'll be Jed," he warned. "Something is wrong with him in the head. You better watch yourself. Somehow you'll have to disarm him, but he's got a houseful of guns."

"Yeah, well, it's not like any law enforcement will be of much help around here. Hedi is here, but she's just one against three," he said. He didn't want to discount Hedi's help, but Jed wouldn't listen to her any more today than he did the last time. Jed didn't respect authority, and he certainly didn't respect women, so Hedi was a double target.

"And he'll shoot you if he sees you," Pete said. "Hedi's dad needs to come."

"Maybe. Call the current sheriff please," Pierce asked.

"I will, but it won't do no good," Pete said. "That sheriff is useless."

"Okay, but you and I both need to call regardless." He hung up the phone from Pete and made a 9-1-1 call to dispatch, telling them exactly what was happening. "If that lousy sheriff of yours doesn't get down here with his deputies, at least this recorded call will be produced when the higher-ups appear, investigating why he didn't do anything. And he'll get charged with manslaughter himself for not stepping in."

The dispatcher gasped. "I don't know who you are, but the sheriff will obviously find out."

"Go ahead and tell him. And your dispatch call had better be recorded. If it's not, you can bet there'll be hell to pay." And he hung up.

He sent Badger a message, letting him know what was going down. This was getting ugly, and it was getting ugly very, very quickly. There was a short and hard response. Something about you do what you need to do. This needs to hit the news stations. And not a bad idea at that. He pocketed his phone and walked to the front door, opened it a crack and called out, "Well, Jed, here we are again, huh?" He shoved the door open and motioned for Ross to step out.

"I'm not walking out there. Jed will shoot me," Ross cried out.

"Jed, Ross wants to leave. You going to let him?"

"Sure enough," Jed said. "Ross, come on out here."

But Ross shook his head. "Don't make me go out there. I tell you that he'll kill me."

"What do I care?" Pierce said. "It'll save us a whole pile of legal fees."

Ross just looked at him, then walked to the couch and sat down. "I'm not leaving," he said. "Outside is crazy land. Inside you guys might be crazy too, but you just might live through this. Out there, there's no way I will."

"Sorry about that, Jed," Pierce yelled. "Ross has decided you guys are crazy, and he wants to stay inside with us."

There was a heavy snort, and a couple guns were fired in the air as Pierce watched Jed and his two buddies pull together. They were talking.

Pierce took that moment to step out on the front veranda, freeing his revolver, holding it up. "Not one of you three are welcome here," he said.

Jed saw him with the handgun and snorted. "What the hell will you do with that little peewee gun?" He raised his rifle, level with Pierce's chest, and fired.

Pierce shot him and dodged left. He knew exactly where he hit him, and, when Jed started to scream, he knew the other two boys would shoot back. But he had already lined up his second shot and warned them, "I don't care which one of you I shoot, but the next guy I'll kill. That first shot of mine was a deliberate attempt to stop Jed from doing anything really stupid. But now I'll take you down."

The two men glared at him, viciousness in their eyes. They were obviously twins, both bald, pug-faced, portly, and packing a hell of a lot of firearms.

They stared at him, and one said, "You know your days are done."

"He shot at me," Pierce said calmly. "It was self-defense. He won't be using that hand ever again though."

The two men went to Jed, who was kneeling on the ground, holding his hand. Pierce knew the bullet had gone up through the bones and pretty well shattered them, blowing apart all the tiny little finger bones. Pierce didn't feel much sympathy. The man was nothing but a renegade. He'd come here with murder on his mind.

The two brothers glared at him. "We will be back," one said, as they all headed to the twins' truck. With the current state of Jed's hand, he shouldn't be driving.

Pierce nodded. "Not a problem. Just knock and come on in. We'll be waiting for you anytime." And he turned his back on them, walking inside, shutting the door.

CHAPTER 8

HEDI WAS STUNNED at how Pierce had taken control of the confrontation. Certainly he'd had full right to shoot Jed, considering Jed was trying to kill him. She'd really like to see Jed thrown in jail for a good twenty years, until he sobered up, until his kids were grown and could safely lead normal lives. It will take them all so long to get over his abuse.

She stepped forward as Pierce closed the door behind him. "Was that wise?" she asked in a low voice.

He stared at her calmly. "I know you don't know me well. But I've seen more than my fair share of assholes like Jed. The type of work I did in the military, we came up against insurgents who would just as soon kill you flat before they even said hello. And, of course, that's the way the world is during war times. But it's not just like war, it's just like bullies. And you get your fair share of those everywhere. You can't back down. Jed won't go away. He'll have to be stopped. This is a setback for them, but now the Billy boys will want justice for Jed. They need to take Jed to the hospital so somebody can attempt to fix his hand. But I highly doubt he'll allow that to happen. He'll grab a bottle and pour some on top of his wound, scream blue murder, feed his own anger and fury, drink the rest of the bottle, and then he'll come back here, firing with his left hand."

"You're right," she said. "That's who Jed is. He won't go down easy."

"You realize that not only has his blood been shed but likely somebody will die tonight, right?"

She pinched the bridge of her nose. "This is well past what I can handle on my job. We need backup."

"Then call it in," he said as he gazed out the kitchen window.

She followed his gaze and saw the dog on the deck, watching them from the open doorway.

"Hello, Salem." His tone was modulated. Salem just looked at him.

"Is she dangerous?" Hedi asked quietly. She took two steps toward Salem. The shepherd's gaze shifted from Pierce to Hedi. "This is really bad timing to bring her into the fold. She's likely to get shot herself," Hedi warned. "Jed will see her, and that'll just spike his temper again."

"Jed has really got a problem with life, doesn't he?"

"He does in a big way," Hedi agreed, studying this man who stepped into this mess yet appeared to handle it easily, as if creating chaos was handling it. "But you could see that right off the bat."

"He's a bully who's been pushing this town around, and the sheriff not only has let him, he's supported him in doing so. I still don't understand why."

"They're family, cousins," Ross snapped. "Are you trying to get me killed?"

Pierce turned a lazy eye toward him.

Hedi almost smiled. "Nobody's trying to get you killed, Ross. You had every right to walk out there at any point in the last couple hours, except when we were going through the material you were trying to steal," she said quietly. "Feel free to go. You can still leave."

"Even if they've left," Ross said nervously, "they'll be looking for me."

"Of course they are. They're looking for supporters, and you're one of them, so they'll be looking at you to stand on their side with a weapon in your hand and to shoot at us." Pierce leaned against doorjamb, his gun still in his hand. "How do you think I'll take that?"

Resentfully Ross just stared at him. "I think you're all crazy. Life was just fine before you got here. Why don't you pack up your goddamn bags and leave again?"

"Life was only fine because you were stealing from your brother, living on his land, and taking advantage of somebody who needed your help and support. Instead all you did was kick him while he was down and grind him into the dirt, taking everything he had, hoping he'd die soon."

Hedi took a step forward, realizing she had a blood war going on here in her community too. "Just stop, both of you. Ross, you know perfectly well you're capable of leaving anytime. Jed won't shoot you. They might want you to join them, but, if you took off and didn't come back, you know they couldn't find you."

He shot her another resentful look. "Who made you boss? The sheriff says you're useless, just a pair of tits on a badge."

"You mean a badge on a pair of tits?" she said. "Do you think I haven't heard that before? Do you see the sheriff here putting a stop to this? No, of course not. He won't get involved. He'll come afterward and look at all the dead bodies, bring out a backhoe and dig a hole. You know he won't put any more effort into it than that." She smiled at him, seeing the nervousness as he understood just how much trouble he was in. "And you also know, if you're part of that ditch full of bodies, you'll get the exact same treatment. He won't go to any trouble to make sure your sorry ass is saved. As far as he's concerned, he wants it all to go away, whatever's the fastest and easiest method."

"Jed will come back here, and he'll light a fire to this place. I heard him talking about it before. He's got gas at his place."

"That's an interesting thing to say," Pierce said. "Because, of course, that's the last thing I'll allow."

"Yeah? And how will you stop it?" Ross said.

"I've got a couple options. For one, I can drain all the gas on his place."

Ross stared at him, his jaw dropping. "You're going to his place? Are you nuts?"

Pierce drew his brows together at the insult. "If I just sit here and wait for the fight to come to me, I'm just sitting here helpless. I'm not into being helpless." He turned to look at Hedi, studied her carefully for a moment while she stared calmly back at him.

"I know what you'll say," she said. "The answer is yes, but it's dangerous."

"You got any better ideas?"

She shook her head. "You'll never find it all. Anything that can cause a fire like that, hell, it doesn't take much. You can just light a match. Pete's place is pretty old, and it's wood."

"And, of course, you don't have any fire trucks here in this part of the county, do you?"

"There's a volunteer fire department," she said, "but they'll be at least half an hour, if not forty-five minutes away."

"In that case, we need to stop Jed. I should have shot out his kneecaps then." He put his hands on his hips and turned around slowly in a circle.

She could see the ideas percolating as he tried to find the best solution.

His gaze landed on Salem yet again. She had dropped into a lying position across the doorway. He smiled at her. "You're doing much better. You're half inside now."

He looked at the subs, opened the second pack, cut it in four pieces and picked up an end piece, working on it while he stood ten feet away from Salem and just talked to her.

Hedi shook her head. "How can you be so calm?"

"Finally somebody's asking questions that make sense," Ross said. "Hasn't it occurred to you that Jed's got a death wish or something? The man's berserk. We know that. It's ridiculous. Jed will come back here, and he'll kill us all."

"Yeah? So what will you do about it?" Hedi asked him. "Just what are you thinking will get you out of this? Because sure as hell nothing at the moment is coming to my mind."

"Somebody," Ross said, "you and/or the sheriff, needs to arrest Jed. Just look at what he's done."

"So now you're talking about arresting him? Are you serious? How does that work?" she asked with a snort. "As far as I'm concerned, you're as much a part of this as Jed and the Billy brothers are. And all of you will be indicted on as many charges as I can write down."

"I haven't done any of this," Ross protested.

She shook her head and stepped forward, grabbed a piece of sandwich. The stomach acids were churning as she tried to figure a way out of this nightmare. As she watched, it seem like Pierce made some kind of a decision.

He approached Salem and stopped just a couple feet

away. She bounced to her feet and backed up, so she was just on the outside of the door. As he took another step closer, Salem growled, a sound deep in the back of her throat that evoked primitive feelings of fear inside Hedi.

She took a step forward, but Salem didn't even look at her. She wasn't a threat compared to Pierce. And that was understandable. Pierce was in a class all his own. Hedi trusted him instinctively, and, because of that, she was fighting that same instinct. She knew better than to trust so easily. Just because he might have been one of those protector types didn't mean he wouldn't go off half-cocked on his own and do something that would cause this mess to blow up even more.

Hell, he already had. Shooting Jed like he had just pushed those men. She knew it instinctively, and she knew Pierce knew it too, which was why he'd done it. She just didn't know if his actions were based on a clear well-thought-out strategy, unlike Jed's.

As she watched, Pierce dropped to his knees in front of Salem, and the dog stopped growling. She looked more confused than anything. He didn't reach out a hand; he just stared at her calmly, steadily. At this point she'd eaten from the dog food bowl he'd placed outside, plus eaten several treats he'd left her.

"Are you sure she's okay, that it's safe to talk to her?"

"Talk is cheap." Pierce's voice was calm, low. "And she already knows that words lie. It's all about actions with Salem."

"That makes sense," she admitted. "But do we really have time for this?"

"Are you in a rush?" he asked. "I'm not planning on going anywhere. But, when it does come down to a fight, I'd like to know she's on my side, not theirs."

Her breath caught in the back of her throat. She hadn't even thought about that. She'd sent Stephen and Roy messages, hoping somebody was on their way out. Stephen sent back a quick message, saying he was manning the office.

She hit Dial on the phone and called him. "What do you mean, you're manning the office?" she said. "We have a hell of a situation developing here."

"Yeah, and that's why I'm manning Central Station," he said calmly. "No way I'm getting out in that shit."

She gasped in outrage. "Stephen, you're a deputy. Get in the vehicle and come out here."

"Nope. You can have my badge before I'll do that," he said. "I promised my wife and girls I'd be going home to them, not that I'll get shot by some crazy-ass nightmare called Jed. Once you said the Billy boys were there, I was out."

"Who are you waiting on to fix this then?" she yelled.

"The law, that's who," Stephen said.

"*We* are the law." She wanted to scream in frustration, but this was the shit she dealt with all the time.

Pierce raised an eyebrow, then just shook his head.

"You have no idea how much we need you."

"Well, you'll have to do without me," Stephen said quietly. "You'll probably have to do without everybody because the sheriff doesn't think he's got any part to play in this whole mess either."

"Don't tell me that he's still sitting there," she said, dread in her voice. "Please tell me that he's on his way to help calm Jed down."

"If he was coming, it would be to arrest Pierce, since he shot Jed without provocation."

"He had provocation," she snapped. "Jed was trying to shoot him."

"Not what Jed told the sheriff."

She pinched the bridge of her nose and groaned. "This is just too unbelievable."

"Not my problem," Stephen said. "As for Roy, he's on the other end of town today. You're on your own."

His tone was so cheerful, she wondered if he wasn't waiting for her to get killed. "Is that you guys' plan?" Her tone turned hard. "Leave me alone in the middle of violence so I get shot and so you don't have to worry about having your job performance upstaged by a woman?"

"If you get shot, it's your fault," Stephen said. "The sheriff told you not to go."

"No, he did not," Hedi cried out. "He told me to handle it."

"Well, then handle it," Stephen barked.

He had such a feigned innocence that she finally realized he really didn't give a shit. "I wonder how your wife will feel when she finds out you wouldn't leave the office to help a fellow officer," she snapped.

"She'll be delighted because at least she knows I'm coming home to her." And just like that he hung up.

She stared at her phone, her mind racing, wondering what the hell she was supposed to do now. And, if she called the sheriff's office one county over, what would be the repercussions for her and her job?

"Please don't tell me that was the entire sheriff's office?" Ross whined.

"Might as well have been," she said glumly. "This is beyond bad news."

"It doesn't make a damn bit of difference to this shit

going on down here." Pierce looked at her. "But it makes a hell of a lot of difference to this town. How is it the sheriff is still in office? And, by the way, I taped that on my cell phone."

She looked at him in horror. "What will you do with it?"

"I'll send it to the big news station, so they can do an investigation on your lovely sheriff's department, and the deputies who turn their back on fellow officers, and sheriffs who would rather stay in their office and spread lies and rumors," he said. He was busy on his phone again.

She stared in fascination as he hit a final button and then smiled at her.

"There. I've sent it out. We'll see how your sheriff feels in a little bit."

"Don't tell me that you did that. Oh, my God! I'll be in so much trouble," she cried out.

"You're either in trouble, or you'll be dead," Ross said. He had come up at her side. "Honestly, I think that's probably what should have happened a long time ago. This is bullshit. What kind of a sheriff is he?"

"Considering you're the one who put him in power," Pierce said, "what do you think?"

"He paid us," Ross said suddenly. "We're all broke. We didn't care either way who was sheriff, so we accepted the money and voted for him."

Pierce slowly straightened and turned to look at him— his phone recording again. "Are you serious?"

Ross nodded. "It wasn't very much, so it didn't really matter."

Hedi felt her stomach sink. "Any idea how many people accepted money to vote for him?"

Ross shrugged. "I don't know. I imagine at least a hundred of us. But maybe not. Some people would have done it for future favors—you know that."

"I do know that." Her voice sounded harsh even to her ears. "I also know he broke a lot of laws doing that."

"I don't think the law matters to your sheriff," Pierce said thoughtfully. He once again sent off several texts.

"Who are you contacting?" she asked, baffled. "Everything I say, you put into a memo and fire it off."

"We have a problem in this town, and somebody needs to clean it up. I just happen to be here."

"You're hardly going to clean it up," Ross said. "You're just here for a night. A drifter doing nothing but causing shit."

"We'll see about that," Pierce said. He turned to look at the doorway.

Her glance followed his.

"Shit," he said.

And she realized Salem had disappeared with the raised voices.

HE STEPPED OUTSIDE and looked around but saw no sign of her. "Damn, that's a setback."

"Who knew Ross would let out a bombshell like that?" Hedi said.

"Everybody knew it," Ross said. "How else would the sheriff have gotten elected?"

"But knowing something and having proof of it is a totally different thing." Hedi rubbed her forehead. "This is just unbelievable."

"Yep, sure is," Pierce said. "It'll be on the news tonight

though." He motioned at the yard, completely unkempt, that hadn't been mowed in ages. "Did you do any cleanup work around here?"

Ross looked at him but didn't answer.

Pierce nodded. "I'll go for a walk," he said, looking back at Hedi. "I wouldn't mind if there was a pot of coffee by the time I get back." And with that, he stepped off the porch steps and headed toward the tree line, one hundred yards off. Inside was an anger rippling through him that he hadn't felt in a long time. To think the sheriff had bought his votes, and his entire department had refused to help Hedi was unbelievable. Pierce didn't need her help. He figured he could handle this just fine. But he also didn't know exactly what he was up against. She did. He'd hate if anything happened to her though. He'd brought this to a head and didn't want her to be a causality of this war.

The fact that her department hadn't come to back her up in any way was just ugly. And that Stephen guy had no business wearing a badge. Pierce would make sure the last thing he did before he left town was to take that badge off him and make sure he booted his ass out of the department. He didn't know about the other guy, but, if he'd taken off in the opposite direction, that was what he'd get too. They were obviously the sheriff's cronies. And how the hell had she gotten her job? He figured maybe the old deputies might have had a hand in it.

As soon as he hit the tree area, he sat down on a log, closed his eyes and tried to calm down his inner center. He already knew he had to still his energy and thoughts in order to go on the hunt.

Silence inside helped with silence outside.

As he sat for a long moment, something cold pressed

against his fingers. His breath caught, and he held it as he waited. The nudge became a little stronger. He opened his hand, and a muzzle was gently placed inside, not moving beyond anything other than his fingers. He stroked Salem's nose and under her chin.

Slowly he opened his eyes. There were a lot of shadows in the trees, and the sun, already clouded over, was starting to go down. Salem stood at his side, so silent, weary, and yet, so proud. He smiled at her and whispered, "Hello there, girl." An ear twitched. "I'm so sorry for the last few months. We'll make sure we get Pete back here."

Her ears twitched again, and she looked up at Pierce with huge chocolate-colored orbs that were wounded and full of distrust. She'd been hurt. She'd been beaten, and the people she'd always depended upon for her very living and her daily training had deserted her. Not by Pete's own fault but by injuries that had sidelined him and, therefore, her.

He blamed Ross for letting the situation go the way it had, but then Ross appeared to be so weak that it was no wonder he couldn't deal with life. He didn't have a clue how. Every decision he made was the easy one.

Pierce's phone rang. He pulled it out, still gently stroking Salem's neck. He moved up to scratch behind her ear. "Hey, Pete. How are you doing?"

"I don't know what to say," Pete said. "Sounds like hell is breaking loose down there."

"Before we get into it, say hi to Salem. She's right here beside me. I've got the phone to her ear."

There were tears in Pete's voice as he called out to Salem. "Hey, girl. I'm coming home soon."

Salem's ears twitched, and she shook her head, looking down at the phone.

"Keep talking," Pierce encouraged. "She's looking at you."

He let the two of them have a moment as Pete gently called to her, and Salem tried to figure out what was going on.

"Any idea how quickly you can come home?" Pierce said.

"The doc said I could probably come in a couple days." There was shock in his voice. "I don't know why I didn't make this happen before."

"We can't get everything modified by then, but I'm sure we can manage something."

"Did you really shoot Jed?" Pete said abruptly.

"Who told you that?"

"My brother called."

"That would have been a lovely phone call," Pierce said, derision in his voice. "He's quite the head case, that guy."

"Yeah, I know. I'm sorry. He is still my brother, but I really don't want anything to do with him now that I know what he tried to take away from me."

"Everything," Pierce said. "He tried to take everything away from you. Don't you forget that. Not only did he try, he did for a while. You were stuck in rehab, while he lorded it over you. He considered this his home, spending your money."

"Yeah," Pete said, his tone vibrating with anger. "I'm not likely to forget that."

"Why did he call you?" Pierce asked.

"To give me an update on Jed. He said that you might get the house burned down."

"You got any insurance on this place?" Pierce asked.

"I do," he said, "but I don't know about arson."

"Don't you worry about it. As long as it's insured for fire, it can be replaced. And I imagine fire is covered because it's pretty standard coverage. I hope they don't burn it down, but I don't know what those Billy boys are like."

"Evil," Pete said. "They're bullies. They're the evilest nastiness you've ever met."

"They'd have to be pretty bad then," Pierce said, "because honestly, I've met some pretty bad men."

"These are right up there with the worst of them," Pete said. "They'll likely start along the fence line and try to burn it."

"Hmm. Interesting thought," Pierce said. "Do you have any big equipment here?"

"There's a tractor. I was trying to get a couple acres into something growable, near the creek, some nearby water source. I was looking at maybe growing some barley or some grains. There's a local distillery not too far away that was looking for some. I had a soil sample tested, and they said it was good for barley."

"Does the tractor have a blade attachment?"

"There are attachments but not sure about a blade. Rakes for sure, rotors. Why?"

"Because the best way to stop a fire is to build a firebreak," Pierce said. "Is your entire property fenced?"

"Yes, it is. There are a couple fences that start at the driveway. If you take sight of both the wooden fences on either side and follow them, you'll see everything is enclosed. I've got these ten acres. That's a lot of land for anybody to drop a match on. And they can just run up the driveway and torch the house itself."

CHAPTER 9

HEDI PUT AWAY the groceries, offered Ross another portion of a sub, which he took without gratitude and sat down at the table, chewing away morosely. She studied his face. "When did you last have a job?"

He shot her a hard look. "I'm not totally useless, you know?"

"I never thought you were," she said. "I can only see what you've done in this last little while though, so I'm looking to see another aspect to your personality."

"I worked at the mill for a few years. I worked in Fort Collins, but affording a home there was hard, so I came back to the mill. Then the mill shut down, and it seems like life from then on completely stopped."

She understood that, and it wasn't the first time she'd heard such a story. "Have you tried for other work around town?"

"Sure," he said, "but it's not like this small town can absorb so many of us when we're laid off."

"No," she said, "but a lot of people moved, and a lot of people commute."

"I didn't do either," he said. "My brother offered me a place. I knew he had been injured, and I thought he was coming back. I thought I was looking after it for him for a few months, and it gave me a place to land while I figured

129

out what I would do. But then I got cozy, and I started to see myself doing this full-time, once I realized he wouldn't get out of that place. Then it seemed like I could start over somewhere else if I could get together enough money."

"But who said he wouldn't get out of there?" she asked, turning to look at him. "None of us ever heard Pete wouldn't come back."

"I don't know," he said, "but the idea came from somewhere. I thought for sure it was from Pete." He stared out the window. "What do you know about this Pierce guy?"

"I know he's more dangerous than Jed," she said simply. "But I believe he's honorable. He's doing this to help Pete and to help Salem."

"Nobody does this shit to help a dog."

"I think you're wrong. Like Pierce and Pete, that dog served our country, so he is trying to make sure she gets more than beaten and abused."

"Good luck to him then. That dog is a killer."

"If she is, it's something you helped make her," she snapped. Then she took a deep breath and asked, "What are your plans tonight?"

He slid a look in her direction but stayed quiet and then shrugged. "I don't know. If I wait until dark, I might be able to head back into town, drive away with my lights off. Maybe they'd let me go, and I'd be good. I won't be coming back, that's for sure."

She leaned against the stove, crossing her arms over her chest, and watched him. "Do you think they'll have a problem with you leaving?"

"If they can get me to be on their side, that's what they'd ideally like," he said. "But I don't want anything to do with them. This will go down badly. Jed is likely to come back and to just start firing through the doors. He won't give a shit who he kills."

"I'm more worried about his wife and kids."

He shook his head. "I heard her girlfriends went to the house and basically kidnapped her and the kids. They headed into town for some big special event, and they were staying overnight."

Relief swept through her. "I'm glad to hear that." She turned to stare toward the living room, her focus on the front door. "We don't want them all injured because Jed is in such an ugly mood."

"He just got his hand shot apart," Ross said sarcastically. "I hardly imagine he's feeling too good."

"He should have gone to the hospital and gotten it taken care of," she said quietly.

"You know he won't. He'll just shoot himself up with some painkillers and booze and come back to get his revenge."

"And then he won't need to worry about a hospital to-morrow," she stated firmly. "If he comes out firing, I'll be firing back, and he'll go to the morgue."

Ross sank back in the chair. "How can the world always be so black-and-white for you?"

"The world isn't always black-and-white," she said, "but you have to watch how much you let that gray line move."

"Mine just never seemed to stay anywhere," he said. "I go to bed thinking this is the right thing to do, and I wake up in the morning feeling like I made the wrong choice, and I need to change it to something else." He looked at the table where one more portion of the sub remained. "Can I have that?"

"That's mine for later," she said. "I'll need it too." She

wrapped it back in the original wrapping and cleared off the rest of the garbage. Then she offered Ross an apple.

He looked at it and frowned. "Don't know when I last had an apple," he said.

"You should try it," she said quietly. "It's better for you than more sandwich."

"And yet, the sandwich is for you, so how is that fair?"

"I bought it," she said, "so that's fair." She didn't bother telling Ross how Pierce had paid for it. She also didn't think Ross would like to hear she thought jail time was in his future. He'd done a terrible thing to his brother.

He sagged back in the chair and took a bite of the apple. "It'll be a long night," he said.

"It probably will be." Her tone was cool and even. "It doesn't matter much. The night will come whether we're here or not."

He hopped to his feet and paced. "I don't want to be here when night falls."

"Too late," she said. "It's already dark out there."

He turned to look out the kitchen window. "Where do you think he went?"

"I don't know," she said. "Probably to walk the perimeter and to see what kind of danger we're up against."

"As long as he's not stupid enough to go to Jed's on his own," he said. "Jed will shoot him as soon as he sees him."

"What makes you think he'll see him?" She highly suspected Pierce's skills were top-notch, and, if he wanted to go after Jed, then he would go after Jed. And maybe it would be better if he did. Jed was coming back after all of them tonight. This needed to end, and it needed to end tonight.

"I haven't seen him in at least thirty minutes." He shifted, walked to the other window and looked out. "Maybe he left."

"Is his truck gone?"

"I don't know." He looked at her in exasperation. "You're the deputy. You should know this stuff."

She gave a half laugh. "What is it you want from me now that you put the sheriff in power?"

He shrugged. "The sheriff caught me when I was broke," he said. "That's really no biggie."

"It is for everybody in this town."

"Well, it wasn't just me who voted him in. Otherwise he wouldn't have made it in," he snapped. "And that's obvious."

"Maybe." She was tired of the conversation and him. "But you need to decide soon if you're leaving."

"You trying to get rid of me?"

"Yes," she admitted. "You're a liability here. You'll mess things up, and we've already got enough problems without you."

"That's not fair," he blasted. He stood up. "I can go now and hopefully make it into town, and nobody will be the wiser."

She nodded, walked toward the front door and opened it. "Don't let the door hit you on your way out."

He glared at her. "You're really not very friendly."

"Nope, I'm probably not," she said. "But it is what it is."

He grabbed the bag from the living room and walked out.

With relief she watched as he got into his truck. He started it up, turned around and headed down to the highway toward town instead of heading toward Jed's.

With any luck he'd stay away, but, with him, you never knew. He could take a back road and circle around. If he was smart, he'd stay a long way away from Jed. What she needed was reinforcements. She needed Jed picked up, along with the Billy boys, but it didn't look like anybody would be around to give her a hand. It figured.

Just then her phone rang. It was her father. "How are you doing, Dad? Are you coming over here?"

"We're taking up stations all around, keeping an eye on the place. I want you to stay inside that house. We'll let you know if we see anybody coming."

"That's nice," she said, "but just remember. You're not the sheriff anymore, and I'm not your deputy."

His voice sharpened. "I get that. You're the one in charge, but we need to make sure these guys don't sneak over your way and catch you unaware."

"Appreciate the extra set of eyes," she said.

"Another thing. Pete called me again." Her father had a note of humor in his voice. "And damn it was good to hear from him. He wants to take a look at what's going on."

"Wow," she said in astonishment. "That's probably a grand idea."

"I think he can. I don't imagine he'll be in great shape, but, if he sees what he's coming back to, it might help him heal faster."

"True enough," she said. "Is somebody going to get him?"

"We're discussing it now. It depends on what happens tonight."

"Anybody talk to the sheriff?"

"That would be a waste of time, as you know," he said. "But I should give him a shout and see what he has to say for himself."

"You do that," she said. "See how the old sheriff meets

up with the new sheriff."

"It hasn't done any good up until now."

"There is one thing we accomplished. Ross said they were all paid to vote for him."

Nothing but silence came through the phone for a few moments. "Are you serious?" her father exploded in outrage.

"Yes. Pierce said something about putting it on the news. I don't know if he meant it or not. He's also got a recording of the deputy saying the sheriff said he wouldn't be bothered coming to help out, and Stephen said he was going home to his wife and kids rather than giving me backup, and Roy had gone to the other side of town so he didn't have to come this direction." She listened as her father swore and cussed up one side and down the other.

"I can't believe they're in power," he said. "That's just too unbelievable."

They talked for a few more minutes. Only as she walked back into the kitchen did she realize Ross had stolen her sandwich as he walked out the door. She snorted and turned to stare at the highway. "Good riddance," she snapped.

She turned toward the countertop and put on a pot of coffee. She didn't know when Pierce would return, but she figured the coffee would be ready when he got here.

PIERCE WORKED THE back forty with the tractor, building a large firebreak. The tractor was old and clunky, but, if nothing else, it was something they could get away in if the other exits were closed off. It would travel across country that many other machines couldn't.

He parked it along the back of the yard, pocketed the

keys and jumped the fence. He walked to where he'd last seen Salem, calling out to her. Almost instantly she approached. She stayed just off to the side, but she was close enough she could see him. He reached into his pocket and pulled out another treat and tossed it at her. She didn't miss it. Her jaws clamped shut, and she kept walking beside him as he headed toward the house.

It was pitch-black outside, and there were no signs of anybody approaching. He'd be on sentry duty all night. He needed coffee to keep himself awake. He knew this would come to a major climax, and he wanted to make sure it came to a favorable one. If Jed was stupid, he'd gone home and wrapped up his hand and was now planning his next visit.

A part of Pierce wanted to go to Jed's house and take him out. But he couldn't handle Jed and the Billy boys if they were all together, and, if they were apart, he couldn't take out one either because he wouldn't know that the other two hadn't come back to Pete's house. Pierce had no problem shooting the Billy boys, but he couldn't do it without provocation.

He could see Hedi moving around in the kitchen. There was just something so welcoming seeing her like that. He respected that she'd come back. Maybe to her it was the job pushing her, and maybe it was because she was worried. It didn't matter; he appreciated the thought. But she was somebody he had to watch out for, somebody he had to make sure didn't get shot. He didn't know if the media had gotten the message about what was going on here yet or about the lousy sheriff, but Pierce's hands were full right where he was, with no time to check whether others were doing their jobs or not.

He looked at Salem and smiled. "You're the reason I'm

here," he said gently.

Her ears twitched at the sound of his voice.

He stopped and crouched down. They were only about twenty feet from the porch, and she walked closer. He reached out a hand, and gently she stretched out her head. He stroked the underside of her chin and neck, gently scratching around her ears. "It's been a tough couple months, hasn't it, baby? That's okay. We'll get through this." And he walked up to the house.

Salem stayed just behind him, her eyes ever-watchful, her body ever-ready.

He hadn't had a chance to check her to see what the blood on her flank was from. He wasn't sure if Jed had given her a parting gift or if it was just an accident while she was out roaming around. She was still favoring one leg, but she appeared to be using it, not letting it slow her down.

He stepped into the kitchen, smelling the coffee. "Perfect timing," he said, his nose in the air.

"Maybe," she said from the shadows by the table. "Ross left."

"Good riddance," he said.

She laughed. "That's exactly what I said."

He grinned at her. "Great minds and all that." He walked to the coffeepot and poured himself a cup. He turned to look at her. "Do you want a cup?"

"Yes, please." She got up and walked toward him.

Now that it was just the two of them and no other distractions except for Salem who stood at the open doorway, he realized Hedi was at least five feet, nine or ten inches, slim, maybe a hundred twenty or twenty-five pounds. She had brown hair that hung down her back. Earlier it had been in a braid and tucked up on the back of her head.

"It's a shame to tie all that hair up in back," he said.

"My father always warned me that it was a weapon for the bad guys, and, when I'm at work, I should make sure it wasn't something that could be used against me."

"He's right," Pierce said. "And how sad that we have to think about things like that."

"Right? I went into law enforcement because I believed in it," she said. "I was raised in it with my father, and I figured for sure I would follow in his footsteps. But I don't know. This last year has been pretty shitty. The first year I was here working with the sheriff wasn't so bad, but he's only gotten worse over time."

"Again it's tough to follow a leader when you have no respect for him." Pierce leaned against the sink, staring out at the darkness beyond the window. "But, when you let guys like that get too big, it's like the rotten core of an apple. You don't really see it until you dig in a little deeper, and then you see how much damage it caused. If nothing else, I want to make sure we get rid of him. Pete needs somebody to stand by him, not somebody who'll throw him to the wolves. And that seems like what your current sheriff would be like."

"I know," she said. "And that's just sad. But I couldn't have worked as a deputy if my dad was sheriff, and I don't think he wants to resume his old job. We need somebody capable. There isn't really anybody around."

"It's not just this town though either, is it?"

"No, we have a collection of towns here, and basically it's the entire county that the sheriff looks after. Only he doesn't travel. Honestly, he goes from home to the coffee shop to the sheriff's office, and that's it."

"Damn shame," Pierce said. "He's got an opportunity to do something really good here, and instead he does absolutely nothing."

She started to open her mouth when a shot was fired through the living room window.

A gas canister.

He shoved her toward the door. "Go out the back door," he said, and he dove for the canister, a kitchen towel over his nose and mouth as he picked up the canister, opened the front door, and chucked it back out. When it landed the second time, it made a small explosion. But he was already back inside with his revolver in his hand, peering through the window. "That had to be a handmade canister," he muttered to himself.

"Yeah. That'll be a Billy boy deal," she said from across the window.

He glared at her. "I told you to go outside."

"Yep, you might have," she said, "but I don't listen to you. As a matter of fact, you're supposed to listen to me."

"Considering I probably have way more experience in this than you do, how about we just not argue about it." He studied the outside intently. "Somebody's behind my truck."

"They'll probably steal the gas from it just for a start," she said. "They do that no matter who's here."

He stared at her a moment. "Wow, this is just a lovely group of people you guys have."

"Not me," she said cheerfully. "The deputy cars are generally safe just because of the sheriff."

He snorted and turned his head. "I'll go out and make sure they don't steal any of my gas."

"And why is that? Are you really prepared to get shot over it?"

"Not at all, but I hope they are." And, just like that, he was outside.

He hoped she'd stayed inside, but he couldn't count on it. She had a mind of her own and figured that she was doing her duty. Maybe she was. He couldn't really hold her back from it. Something he admitted he admired.

He crept around the side of his vehicle, saw another shadow and waited. Then he slipped alongside the fence, keeping his body still at every chance. Finally seeing one of the Billy boys up against his truck, doing something with the gas tank, he stepped up, threw an arm around his neck, choking off his air, and pulled him to the ground.

Against his ear he whispered, "Are you stealing gas or are you pouring sugar in my gas tank?"

The trouble was, he wasn't about to release his arm around his neck to let the asshole answer. He was just way too busy keeping him down. With him flat on the ground and groaning, Pierce closed his gas tank and tied the man's hands with a zip tie he'd stuffed in his pockets earlier. He grabbed a part of the man's T-shirt, ripped it off and stuffed it in his mouth. And then, just for good measure, he gave him a hard clip on the jaw, knocking him out cold.

He had to weigh at least two-forty, if not two-eighty, and Pierce thought about the pros and cons. Then he realized the only way to make sure he would not come back after them was if he was kept inside, tied up, under guard.

Taking a chance, groaning lightly under the heavy weight, he picked up the unconscious man, threw him over his shoulder and raced around to the back.

Once he was inside, the lights all off, Hedi whispered, "Who did you bring with you?"

"One of the twins," Pierce said. "He's tied up at the moment. I'll lock him up somewhere."

"Is that wise?"

"It's wiser than leaving him out there to come back after us," he said. "I don't know about you, but, once I put these guys down, I don't want to have to do it again."

"Good point," she said. "Find me some more rope, will ya? He's not tied secure enough for my peace of mind."

Pierce dropped him on the living room floor, and, with the rope, they hogtied him with his feet up to his hands, placing a bandanna around his jaws to keep the cotton stuffed in his mouth. Pierce faced her and said, "If he wakes up, knock him out again." And he took off back out into the darkness.

CHAPTER 10

H EDI WATCHED PIERCE disappear into the shadows and shook her head. "What the hell am I doing here?"

Well, trying to uphold the law for one and to help out somebody in trouble. But Pierce was a bit of a lone ranger and appeared capable enough to handle this all on his own. So again—why was she here?

She walked back to the prisoner and bent down. "Well, Billy, this is a hell of a pickle."

She checked his bonds to make sure he wasn't going anywhere, then emptied his pockets. She wanted to make sure nothing in them could free himself. With him out cold, she took a picture of his face and sent it to the sheriff.

"One down," she snapped.

She got a response immediately as her phone rang. "What the hell are you doing?" the sheriff roared.

"After Jed and Pierce got into a shootout earlier, and you walked away, the Billy boys came back looking for trouble. Pierce caught Billy siphoning gas out of the truck."

"What? So he siphons off a couple bucks' worth of gasoline. Is that worth knocking him out cold and tying him up? You guys are the ones skirting the law now."

She gasped in disbelief at his words. "Are you serious? Ross said Jed and the Billy brothers are threatening to burn down Pete's place. And you know they're gunning for Pierce.

Do you even care?"

"Why should I care?" the sheriff said calmly. "He's a stranger. He's a nobody."

"But he's protecting somebody who's part of this community," she snapped. "Pete's coming back, and this is his place. He needs our help making sure nobody rides rough-shod all over it."

"You're the one who says Pete's coming back," the sheriff snapped. "You and that lover boy of yours."

She stiffened at the reference to Pierce. "Hardly," she said sarcastically. "You're the sheriff. You should be here keeping Jed and the Billy boys back."

"According to Jed and the Billy boys, your friend attacked them without provocation. So when I come out in the morning, it'll be to arrest Pierce."

She snorted. "Well, good luck with that," she said. "He's got friends in high places."

"Sure he does. That boy is all talk. You've always been an easy mark for the men. Offer you a few flowers and a cup of coffee, and you lie down for any of them," he sneered.

She was horrified that he'd go down that path. "You are out of line." Her voice was hard. "And that's not appropriate behavior between colleagues."

"You *were* a colleague," he said. "But I've just fired you, so you're nobody now." And with that he hung up.

She stared down at her phone in disbelief. "Fired?" For some reason that had never occurred to her. He had a right to fire her, but he had to have a reason. Did he in this case? She wasn't going against his orders. He hadn't ordered her to come back. He hadn't ordered her to leave the place alone. He hadn't ordered her not to get involved. She had citizens here in trouble, and she was trying to help out.

She sent her father a text. **Apparently helping out Pierce and Pete just got me fired.**

Her father texted back. **Sorry, kiddo. Not surprised. Your sheriff doesn't like anybody who goes against his wishes.**

And yet, technically he never told me not to do this. So I'm not sure what he's firing me over. Of course he made a lot of nasty innuendos about me and Pierce.

That's the level he operates at. If he doesn't have anything specific to blame you for, he'll find something. And, in this case, it'll be an inappropriate relationship causing you to overstep your boundaries.

She ran a hand through her hair and wondered what the hell she would do now. Life had gone into an absolute spiral since she'd met Pierce.

She glared out the window, pocketing her phone. "Well, Pierce, is this what happens? Do you inspire a reign of chaos everywhere you go?"

Ross was gone; one of the Billy boys was tied up; Jed was injured, and Pierce was out there with Salem. And she was stuck inside. What the hell was she was supposed to do with that?

Not liking any of her options, she slipped out the back door and wandered down the porch to take a look into the shadows. Her car was in the barn. She needed to go home, pick up the deputy's car and take it back to the station. By now the sheriff would have told Stephen and Roy. They'd both be smirking and saying they'd told her that her actions would get her fired. Not that they had, but, of course, they'd be all about kissing up to the sheriff for firing her. A paycheck was a paycheck in this town where so many businesses had gone under. She had a little money saved, so she was good for a bit, but obviously she'd now have to consider moving. She stepped back inside and headed to the living room to peer out from behind the curtains. Still no sign of anything or anyone.

Just then a text came back from her father. **Just got a phone call from your mom. Something about this blowing up all over the news.**

She brightened. Instead of trying to text an answer, she called him. When he answered on the first ring, she said, "Pierce said he would contact the media."

"Good," he said. "I've already tried to contact the higher-ups, but everybody wants to leave the sheriff to do his job."

"You know what that's all about," she said. "But, in this instance, the sheriff is just waiting for the dust to die down. Then he'll come in and make it look like he made it all happen—or not—depending on the outcome. He doesn't let anybody take the glory away from him, and neither will he put himself in danger or get his hands dirty."

"Where are you now?"

"I'm at the back of the house," she said. "Pierce took off into the shadows, and I have no clue what he's up to. Of course, I have Billy here tied up. Ross slipped away earlier, but honestly, I don't know if we can trust him. He could just as easily have gone to Jed's."

"Your mom contacted Vicky. She and the kids are okay. They're at her mom's. Your mom is trying to convince her not to go home. I'm not sure it'll take very much convincing after this. She's pretty scared."

"The only thing is, she needs her job," Hedi said sadly. "And he'll find her there."

"Yeah, true enough. The sheriff won't arrest Jed for beating on his wife and kids. He sure as hell won't arrest Jed for going after a guy who shot him."

"No, but Jed was going to kill Pierce, and I can attest to that."

"Chances are you'll have to," her father warned.

"It was all in the line of duty. But I'm no longer an official officer of the law." Her tone had turned hard. "So I guess right now I'm just a private citizen helping a friend."

"Just a question on that," her dad asked. "Which friend?"

"At this time, both of them," she said softly. "There's a lot to like about Pierce. He's a good man. He also stood up for me against Jed, beat Jed down for hurting his kids. No doubt Pierce's one of the good guys. But he's only here for a short time, and then he's taking off again."

"Too bad," the ex-sheriff said. "Sounds to me like he'd make a great sheriff."

She laughed at that. "I don't know," she said. "He's pretty unbridled."

"What the job needs is somebody who knows when it's time to act and who knows when it's time to sit back. So far we've seen he knows when it's time to act. The question now is, is he astute enough to recognize when it's time to sit back?"

"I don't know," she said, "but, as I'm no longer here on behalf of the law, I'm feeling a bit at loose ends."

"You want to stay?"

"Yes," she said, her tone sharp. "I'll finish what I started. Besides, without me, Pierce has no backup."

"Me and the boys are out here," her father said. "You can either join us or you can stay where you are. But you do need to confirm either way with us, so we know to look for you when shadows start moving."

"I'm here at the house," she said. "I want to do a full search on the outbuildings. But remember Pierce is out in the shadows. I don't know where. Not even sure what he's after."

"If he's smart, he'll have gone to Jed's house to see if they're there."

"Maybe," she said. "But I don't know where Jed is. He should have gotten that hand looked after."

"It depends on how drunk he is. Right now he won't be feeling any pain. It'll just be that same old festering anger, only now he has a specific target," her father warned. "I'm sorry for Pete. It seems like he's the one caught in the middle of all of this."

"He is, indeed," she said. "I'd love to see him come back sooner rather than later—get his input on the renovations."

"I hear you. But that's out of my hands. If Pete calls me for a ride, I'll be the first one to go get him. Hell, maybe I'll call him and offer him one first."

On that note she hung up. She stood for a few moments, then slipped outside, listening to the silence around her. There hadn't been anything while she'd been talking, but it was so easy to miss a sound.

Taking a chance, she slipped to the fence line and crept around to the barn. As soon as she stepped inside, the air felt different, staticky with expectancy. And she knew she wasn't alone.

JED'S HOUSE LOOMED large on the left. Pierce leaned against a tree and studied it. Jed was out front beside a pickup— looked like a reject from the junkyard—swearing and cursing at something. Then that seemed to be all he did besides drinking and abusing people and Salem. Jed might have been a good man in his heyday, but circumstances and the bottle had dragged him down, way down.

There was no way to make heads or tails out of his words either, but apparently the truck wouldn't start. No surprise there. A providence that Pierce would look on with a smile. He couldn't be sure what Jed's plan was, but it likely wasn't anything decent.

Just then Jed turned and stumbled back to the house, and Pierce meant *stumbled*. Jed could barely keep himself upright. He'd obviously come home and consumed the better part of a bottle. He held a propane torch canister in his hand, which also didn't say much good about what was going on in his head. He made it inside the door, slamming it behind him. Once again words filled the air, but they were just the same repeated swear words from before.

Pierce slipped up to the corner of the house and peered in the window. Jed appeared to be alone. He was pouring a slug back from the bottle that only had a couple inches left on the bottom. When he ran out, if he did run out, then things would get ugly yet again. Jed would need a steady influx of that booze to keep him going, to fuel his anger, to numb his gunshot wound. Either that or it would knock him out. But he had a huge tolerance. So many alcoholics could function at levels that would knock out normal individuals.

Pierce studied Jed as he moved around the house, knocking papers off the table and dumping chairs to the side. He was trying to light the propane torch in his hand with a sparking fire, trying to get it to give him a few inches of flame. It was an accident waiting to happen. Jed swore again when it wouldn't light. This time Pierce sighed with relief.

When something cold nestled his hand, he jumped slightly and turned to look down. "Well, Salem, you are one sneaky dog," he whispered. He crouched lower and gently stroked her head.

She looked at him with those huge eyes, worried she was trusting the wrong man yet again.

He brushed his hand down the back of her neck, scratched her ruff and said, "How are you doing, huh? You shouldn't be over here. This is one guy who'll torture you and watch you burn alive."

She seemed to understand his words because she shot a hesitant look toward the house.

He straightened, peered in the window and saw Jed coming around to the rear kitchen door. Calling Salem to him with hand signals, Pierce raced back to the tree, the two of them blending into the fence in the woods. He watched from a distance as Jed tripped out the back door, standing there cursing the moon, shaking a fist at the sky. Pierce wondered at the anger that drove this man. And then he heard Jed speak.

"Goddammit, Vicky. Get your fucking ass back home again. I'm hungry. A man needs to eat, you know?"

Pierce's eyebrows shot up. So he was upset about Vicky. He saw a phone in Jed's hand and realized Jed was talking. Then he smashed the phone against a fence post. A shot Pierce didn't think Jed could make, except for the fact that he was drunk. And somehow drunks seemed to have the luck.

"Goddamn bitch. No way you get to leave me," he roared.

That made more sense. Vicky was gone, and here Jed was. That was the last straw for him. And just like that, he fired up that spark to get the torch to light, and, indeed, it did.

Out came a good foot-long shot of flame. And that had Jed laughing like a loon. He shut down the burner again, lit it once more to make sure it worked once more, and then walked around the house toward his junkyard truck.

Pierce knew the real trouble had just started. They were heading into a full-blown war right now, and it was one nobody would win. His first priority was to avoid loss of life. The second priority was to avoid loss of property. And the only property he gave a shit about was Pete's.

Seeing Jed get into the truck and manage to start it up, put it in gear and reverse it down the driveway had Pierce racing back toward Pete's property. With Salem running free at his side, the two matched pace for pace with the truck on the road. At least the driveway would take some twists and turns, whereas Pierce cut across the back forty and would be there, hopefully, at the same time.

CHAPTER 11

B ACK IN THE house, Hedi saw Billy lying on the floor, staring up at her, absolute hate in his gaze. She crouched and said, "Oh, I'm sorry you're awake. You're much easier to deal with when you're unconscious."

"So are you," he mumbled around the cloth in his mouth, glaring at her.

She ignored him, knowing he was very much of the opinion a woman should be available whenever a man wanted, and it didn't matter if she was willing or not. She walked to the front door and stared out. Her knees were weak from her damn fast mad dash back from the barn, but now she knew that was where the danger was. Only one handgun did not an army make.

Hating to be inside, she walked back to the kitchen and slipped out into the darkness. Instantly she felt better. She hated that she'd run away from the evil presence in the barn and wondered at the sense of going back in again. Was Bobby there? If so, she wasn't ready to take him on, not on her own. Not when she didn't know where Jed was.

She checked out the lay of the land, slipped to the right, away from the barn, caught up with the fence and crept along the side so she was between the barn and the house where she had a better vantage point. A copse of trees was there, and she could hide a little easier.

From that point she crouched down low and watched. When her phone buzzed in her hand, she took a look and read the message from Pierce. "Shit, shit, shit," she snapped. This was so not cool.

She forwarded the text to her father, adding, **Jed is liquored up and running around with a working blowtorch.**

She could only hope her father and his men stopped Jed before he got here and caused any more trouble. If ever there was a mangy dog that needed to be put down, it was Jed.

In the last two years of being a deputy her job had been pretty damn easy. She'd learned a lot from her father and less than nothing from the current sheriff. She wondered if tonight's media hype would cause a kerfuffle. Or would it garner only a brief mention and disappear like so many other incidents? She really wanted the sheriff gone but didn't know how to make that happen.

Waiting for something to happen was interminable. Five minutes became ten. Where was Jed? He should be coming any moment. And whoever was in the barn, what were they doing? Just waiting for Jed to show up?

In the distance she could hear an owl's long cry. She turned to look up but didn't see any owl.

Her eye caught a sign of movement. She twisted slightly to spot Pierce motioning at her several trees behind her. She nodded, took a careful look around and then crept low along the grass. There was no way to make it, fast or slow, and not be noticed. There just wasn't enough here for total ground cover. If she was lucky, whoever was in the barn was deep in the barn and not looking out the double doors.

When she reached Pierce's side, she hunkered down and whispered, "What the hell's going on?"

"Jed is gunning toward murder and arson," he said. "I was hoping our backup would come a little faster."

"My father, Roger, and Stew, one of his former deputies, are here," she said. "They're hoping to stop Jed before he gets here."

"Somebody has to," he said. "Jed is just a live wire. He's on a rampage. I think he got a call from his wife saying she was leaving him."

"Oh, shit. That would be really bad timing on her part," Hedi said.

"And sent Jed, who was already on the edge—or rather over the edge—completely off the cliff," Pierce said.

Her phone rang. "Dad, what's up?"

"Jed is one cagey drunk. He must have seen us without us seeing him," he said. "When he didn't show up on the roadway as soon as we expected, we went looking for him. Found his abandoned truck—that second work truck of his—parked off-road. He left it and obviously took off on foot. We checked his ride, specifically for the torch. And, yeah, he still has it."

"So he could already be here," she said, looking around the area. "I think somebody's in the barn. It's probably Bobby, waiting for Jed to show up."

"Make sure you don't go back in that barn or the house," her father ordered.

"I'm out in the trees with Pierce. He also said he heard part of a conversation with Jed about maybe Vicky leaving him."

"If that's the case," her father said, "nobody is bringing Jed in tonight. He'll take out as many as he can, including himself. But, if he doesn't get stopped here, you know he'll be going after his wife next."

"Please get her someplace safe," she told her father urgently.

"I'm sending Stew to Vicky and the kids. He'll watch over them, even move them if he has to."

Hedi nodded. "Those kids have been through enough already. We can't have Jed taking them all out just because he's pissed."

"He's been pissed for a long time," her father said. "Make sure you're not a target of Jed's rage tonight."

"Not planning on that, but someone needs to stop him. And I want to make sure we take down Bobby in the barn, if that's who's there," she said. "I just can't be sure it is." She turned to look at Pierce.

He held a finger to his lips and disappeared in front of her.

"Pierce is about to confirm who's in the barn," she said. "And, if Jed sets Pete's house on fire, he'll burn up Billy. That'll just be another shitstorm."

"Don't go back inside that house," her father repeated.

She hung up the phone, pocketed it and slipped back through the trees, around to the barn, watching Pierce creep up close. The barn had double doors on this side, and a single door and window on the back. She never understood why barns didn't come with multiple windows so you had better access and better light, but apparently they didn't. At least not during the time that this one was built.

As she watched, Pierce sneaked up to the double doors and waited. There wasn't a sound. She wanted to tell him to stop, not to even bother, that they could wait Bobby out. Then they could just watch and keep track as Bobby tried to leave. But Pierce didn't appear to be the waiting kind of guy because, even as she watched, he disappeared inside the barn.

PIERCE STUDIED THE interior of the barn. He was as low to the ground as he could get, tucked alongside the wall and hunkered under a saddle stand with a big old leather saddle on top. He listened with his eyes closed and his ears wide open, and he could hear feet shifting impatiently on the left at the back. Whether he'd been seen or not, he didn't know. The barn was too dark at the moment, and he hadn't been here long enough to have the lay of the land. Chances were good Bobby knew the interior better than Pierce did.

As he waited, the back door opened, and somebody stumbled inside. "Bobby, you there?"

Bobby whispered, "Yeah. What took you so long?"

"A roadblock was out there for me. Had to walk the last part."

"A roadblock? The sheriff? No way, man. That's what we pay him for."

"Well, we didn't pay him enough because there's at least one truck if not two or three."

"Could have just been somebody broke down," Bobby said.

"I don't know. It doesn't matter. I got the torch."

"We didn't have to have a torch. We needed gasoline. We could take it from her car but we might need that as a getaway vehicle."

"That's what Billy was supposed to get. Where is he?"

"No idea," Bobby said, his voice hard but fretting. "Last I saw he was getting gas from the truck, but I never saw him again."

"Goddamn fucking shit," Jed roared. "It's gotta be that asshole."

"Yeah, I think you're right," he said. "But I don't want to torch the house until I know if my brother is in there."

"We're torching the house," Jed said. "If your brother is in there, goddammit, he better get his ass out fast."

"I don't know if he's alive or not," Bobby said. "But I'm not killing him if he's unconscious or if he's tied up and can't leave."

"We'll run out of options pretty damn soon," Jed said. "And I'm not waiting around for the roadblock assholes to get here."

"What do you want to do?" Bobby asked.

"I want to go in. We'll start the fire between the barn and the house and do a quick run-through of the house. If Billy is there, we'll get him out. But nobody else gets to leave. We'll shoot them if they try."

CHAPTER 12

S HE WATCHED AS Pierce slipped back out the door and crept along the high grass to the back. She could only imagine what he was doing because she certainly couldn't see. Then he came back around to the front and in a move that surprised her, he closed both front double doors and threw a board across them. She raced down to meet him. "You locked the men in?"

He nodded. "Their plan is to burn the place down." He held up his phone. "I recorded it all."

"Oh, wow, that's incredible."

"Not really," he said. "In normal circumstances, the sheriff would arrest these guys for attempted arson, not to mention trespassing, breaking and entering, and any number of other nasty things. In this case, we've got calls out to the other counties' sheriffs close by. One is on his way. One contacted your sheriff, and he said he's got a madman running loose, being me I presume, and that's the way it goes," he said with a half shoulder shrug. "Fort Collins has a police department, and they've been alerted to the problems. Give me a minute, and I'll send this recording to them." He sat down with his back against the barn door and started to text.

She squatted beside him, and, just as she lowered herself down, a bullet came flying from inside the barn door right where her head had been. "Shit," she said and hit the ground flat. That had been close, too damn close.

"We can expect them to keep that up too," he said. "Let's get a safe distance away."

They made their way back to the trees, where they could watch both ends of the barn.

"They'll try to come out through the window," he said, "but it's pretty high and small, or they will open the front doors by shooting their way out."

"And then what?"

"I'd love to set a trap for them," he said, running his hand through his hair as he studied the barn. "Or I can just make it so they can't get out. That sounds like a better idea to me." And he took off across the yard toward his truck. There he started it up and drove down to the end of the lane, where Jed had dropped off his beloved truck for his previous visit, before he got shot in his gun hand.

She watched, wondering how he would start it, when all of a sudden it came trembling toward the barn. She shook her head, wondering at the madness of this night as Pierce pulled Jed's truck up sideways and parked right in front of the double doors so that he had to crawl out the passenger side in order to get out. She watched as the back door rattled, and bullets shot through it. The window was shot out, and broken glass shattered everywhere.

"Don't do that," Jed roared. "We'll get cut on the way out."

"I ain't getting out that way anyway," Bobby said. "That window ain't big enough for me."

She wanted to laugh, but it was such a bizarre night she didn't dare. She stayed hunkered low, keeping watch. Bullets flew out in all directions, as if one of them stood in the center of the room and just started shooting, hoping to hit somebody on the outside.

When the shots slowed down, Pierce called out. "You're firing into Jed's truck. It's parked at the double doors."

"What the hell?" Jed exploded. "You leave my truck alone."

"Not my fault if you shoot it," Pierce said. "When you run out of ammo, let me know, and I'll open the door for you."

Immediately a barrage of gunfire headed in the direction of his voice. But Pierce was no longer there. She shook her head and sat down to wait. Pierce was right; at some point they would run out of ammo.

But she knew these men. They came prepared for bear. They could also burn down the barn and her car with it. And just then she realized Pierce had thought of the same thing. Because without a word, he went racing behind her, flat out to the back.

She stood up. "What the hell ..."

But he didn't answer.

The next thing she knew, he slowly drove the tractor toward her. She frowned as he built a massive firebreak around the barn so that, if they did light the barn on fire, it would collapse in on itself and not spread to any other buildings around it.

She looked up at the trees. A couple branches could catch fire but not many. She had no idea how much value was in that barn itself, but it was a hell of a lot better to lose that than to lose the house.

As soon as Jed and Bobby heard the tractor outside, she figured they'd start shooting again. Pierce stopped when he got close to the barn, his firebreak a good six to eight feet away, and studied the barn for a long moment. He didn't trust them, and she didn't blame him.

He got off the tractor and picked up a piece of sheet metal lying on the ground. He propped that up beside him in the tractor cab, then with a hand on the top, he slowly completed the round of firebreak closer to the barn, with that sheet metal hopefully protecting him from any bullets coming through the barn. Then he went to his truck, rummaged in the back and came up with a handsaw. Next thing she knew, he shimmied up the tree overhanging the barn, cutting down branches. Obviously he took the fire pretty damn seriously. But she grinned, loving his chutzpah.

When he joined her, huffing slightly, a bead of sweat on his forehead, she whispered, "You're a handy man to have around."

He leaned over and kissed her hard and fast. "Sweetheart, you have no idea."

She chuckled at that. "Does that line actually get you somewhere with women?" she asked, trying to ignore the kiss. She'd been right when she had told her father that Pierce was a good man to have around in time of need. She figured he was one of the good guys, period.

A hell of a lot of banked fire was in that kiss. And damn she wanted to taste his lips again.

"Since we'll need a new sheriff," she said in a conversational tone of voice, "you looking for a job?"

He looked at her in horror. "You wouldn't saddle me with that, would you?"

She raised her eyebrows. "It's an office of respect. It's men upholding the law." She motioned toward the barn. "Personally I think you'd be great."

"The position isn't open anyway," he said amiably. "So I

don't have to worry about it."

"Maybe not," she said, "but you should. Apply, at least."

"Again, no open job, remember?"

"I also believe in the law," she said, "so I have to believe this sheriff will get his ass booted out somehow or another, and there will be an open position."

"What about you?" he asked. "Do you want the job?"

She shook her head. "Nope. I'm happy as support staff. It's not that I can't do the job, but I don't have the attitude you do. At the office, as it stands now, I'm the most aggressive one there, and that's damn sad. Since I met you though, I realize you're very much like my father, so I'm a good person to back you up. But I'm not necessarily the right person to lead."

He studied her for a long moment and smiled. "I'll take your lead any day."

She groaned and shook her head. "Stop the sexual innuendoes."

"Why?" he said. "I was just getting started."

"Wow," she said. "How did this come out of the blue?"

"Hasn't been out of the blue," he said with a smirk. "I know solid gold when I see it."

She stared at him in surprise. "Me?"

It was his turn to stop and look at her. "Absolutely you. Surprised?"

She nodded.

"YOU SHOULDN'T BE," he said briskly wondering why she would be. "You can tell an awful lot about a person in a scenario like this. Look at all the characters involved, and who is it who stands up straight on the side of right?"

"Just you and me and Dad and Roger and Stew from what I can see," she said.

"Exactly. You're solid gold. You were there earlier, pushing back at Jed when he was trying to hurt those kids. You came here to help me because I was trying to help Pete," he said. "You stuck around because you knew it was the right thing to do. Solid gold. The fact that you're also a looker and have a personality that balances nicely with mine only helps."

"That is not a relationship."

He twisted, looked at her and grinned. "No. But we could try."

"Try what? A relationship?" she asked drily. "You flash into town, and next you'll be flashing out of town."

"No. Probably not. I might not be able to do all those renos for Pete, but I can sure get a handle on most of them. If I need tradesmen, we'll take a look at that cost then," he said. "Hell, I might even know enough guys to help out myself. And most of them would be happy to help a fellow vet."

"Then you know the right kind of men," she said sadly. "It seems like all I've been surrounded by is these guys." She motioned at the barn. "Or the two deputies I work with and the sheriff."

"Definitely time for housecleaning," he said. Just then he caught sight of Salem. "Don't say or do anything now, but Salem is coming up between us."

She looked at him in shock. "I forgot about her."

"I haven't. She was with me every step of the way back from Jed's, and then I told her to stay in the trees. I did not want Jed to get a chance to shoot her."

"Or burn her alive," Hedi said sadly. "He's just that kind

of guy."

"I think I told her that too," he said with a chuckle. He looked down and held out his hand. Salem walked into it. He spent a moment gently stroking her forehead and the back of her neck. She was gentle and loving, and it angered him at a deep level to see how she'd been treated.

Hedi watched the two of them. "She really likes you, doesn't she?"

"I haven't starved her. I haven't made her do something against her nature. And I treat her with respect and love. What's not to like?" Hedi looked at him for a long moment, and he wondered what she was thinking.

"It's just that easy, isn't it?" she asked. "Jed did treat her badly. He never once treated her with respect or love. Just like he never treated his wife and kids with respect or love."

"Vicky was a prisoner, an abused one at that," he said shortly. "A man has got no business beating up on a woman. You guys can't fight back the same. You don't have the meanness we have, and you don't have the strength. And, if you're in a marriage, you're there because you want to be, at least at first because there's respect, there's love, and because there's a commitment," he added gently.

"Too bad it doesn't work out that way most times," she said gently.

"Ever been married?" he asked.

"No," she said. "I came close a time or two, but, in one case, a local job fell through for him, and I realized I didn't love him enough to leave here." She gave Pierce a crooked grin. "Unfortunately it took me a little too long to figure that out."

"Better late than never," he said. "Imagine if you had gotten married and had two kids, *then* realized how unhappy you were?"

"I was also very young, two months short of my eighteenth birthday. And I just wasn't ready."

"That is young," he said. "And the other incident?"

"Somebody I thought would be the one." An evident note of bitterness filled her voice. "But apparently a half dozen other girls thought the same thing."

"Ouch," he said. "Yeah, that's the other kind of relationship. I don't do those."

"What do you mean, you don't do those?"

"Multiple partners," he said. "When I commit, I commit fully. And I demand commitment on both sides. Life is full of diversions. You choose what you'll focus on and go after what you truly want. Otherwise you can expend your energy on too many things, and you get nowhere quickly."

"Sure, but a marriage isn't exactly a goal that you have to work toward."

"I think it is," he said. "Relationships are goals. Every single day you get up, and you work on your relationships to make them the best damn relationships you can have." He stared up at the night sky. "I don't understand how people can just fall into a relationship and stay there, even though it's no good."

"You have a very unique view on life," she said slowly. "But I like it." In fact, it gave her great insight into who he was.

"Yeah, probably from being in the military, going through rehab, recovering from injuries, all that good stuff," he said.

"I can't see anything wrong with your viewpoint," she said. "It seems like honesty, integrity, morality, ethics, they're all something that's becoming old-fashioned and falling out of favor."

"No. You just had a tainted view for the last few years because the people you work with suck," he said, startling a laugh from her.

"I hear you there," she said, "but I'm really glad you don't suck."

"See? That's what I mean. We click."

"Clicking is not a relationship," she reiterated, but he was getting to her, intriguing her at the same time he was mystifying her. One of the most interesting men to come into her world.

"No, but it's a good basis for one," he said.

Just then a bullet was fired in their direction. They both hunkered lower, and Salem started to growl. Pierce placed a hand on her shoulder. "Easy, girl." He studied the darkness. "Did that come from inside the barn?"

"I'm not sure it did," she said. "They might have kicked out part of the back wall and snuck around on us."

"It's all too possible," he said almost philosophically.

Salem growled again deep in the back of her throat.

"She really doesn't like these guys, does she?" asked Pierce. "But we can't watch four sides at once."

"I know," she said. "But I really don't want to see them get out before our backup arrives."

"I'm not sure where the backup is," he said. "Chances are it'll be a little far away yet."

"Dad and Roger are out there, keeping an eye out. But we should have others coming too," she said. "We put out the call at least an hour ago."

"Maybe."

Just then more shots were fired in their direction. Salem growled yet again. Pierce put a hand on her fur to calm her down.

"She doesn't like gunfire, does she?" Hedi asked Pierce.

"No. When she was attacked with Pete, insurgents had opened fire. I'm sure she associates that gunfire with what happened to her life and to Pete."

Hedi gasped. "That's terrible."

"Unfortunately it's all too common. Dogs are almost human in many ways."

The gunfire increased, a heavy barrage that kept their heads lowered.

"We're sitting ducks," he said. Quietly he grabbed her hand. "Follow me."

And just like that they were up and racing away, Salem at his side as they went deeper into the woods. Bullets fired in their direction once more.

"We can assume they escaped the barn," she gasped.

"Yep, they're out and free, or they have backup."

"Who would that would be?"

"It could be any number of people, but I see two possibilities."

"Who?" she cried out.

"Either Billy, who we left tied up inside the house, or … Ross."

CHAPTER 13

S HE HATED TO concede he had a point, but it was valid. "If it's Ross, he parked somewhere out of sight and walked."

"He probably parked at Jed's and walked in. He could have released Billy, and now we've got both of them after us."

"Shit," she said. She picked up her phone and called her father. "Did you see anyone on foot?"

"No," he said slowly. "Roger said he thought he saw a shadow, but, when he went to investigate, no one was there."

"We're under heavy gunfire," she murmured. "We had two of them pinned in the barn, Jed and Bobby, but now we're in the trees running away from the house."

"You stay hidden," her father ordered.

"You be careful, Dad," she snapped. "There's likely four now, all heavily armed. At this point, I want the bloody National Guard."

He chuckled. "You won't get that, but you will get us. And we do have word that Fort Collins is on its way. They're about ten minutes out."

At the mention of *ten minutes*, her heart gave a sigh of relief. "We can handle ten minutes, or rather I can." She turned to look around to see Pierce already gone, Salem at his side. "Pierce and Salem are heading back toward the house and the barn, so I don't know that they can."

"Get them to stay where you are," her father cried out in alarm.

"Not happening, Dad. He's already too far gone for that. Get here as soon as you can. I'm going after him." And she wasted no time pocketing her phone, racing behind Pierce. She wasn't at all sure what he was up to, but she knew he wouldn't go down without a fight, and she wouldn't let him go down alone.

Swearing silently under her breath, she came up to a copse of trees where she could see the house clearly and almost cried out in surprise when a hand smacked around her mouth.

Pierce whispered in her ear. "You should have stayed behind."

She shook her head, brushing off his hand. "What, and let you run off and have all the fun?"

His white teeth flashed in the dark. "Hardly, but at least here I don't have to worry about somebody circling around and back again."

"No," she said, "you don't. On the other hand, I'm not sure that's any help." Then she passed on her father's message.

Together the two walked to the edge of the copse where they could see the house. He looked at it and said, "I don't want Pete to lose that house."

"I don't think we have any choice," she said. "There are too many bad guys. Better the property than our lives. And definitely can't lose Salem. Pete needs her."

"I want you to stay here," he said. "There might be four of them loose now, but I can knock that number down to half. There's a good chance I can take their weapons, and that'll give us a decided advantage."

"What can I do to help?"

He leaned over and kissed her again. "See? That's what I mean. Just the right kind of attitude."

"Not quite," she said. "I don't want to get shot, and whatever you're planning on doing is likely to get us both in that condition."

"No," he said cheerfully. "That's not on my agenda. What I want you to do is stay here for five minutes. When you hear an owl call, come toward the call."

"How will I know where that is in the darkness?" she asked.

But, once again, he was gone, Salem a mere shadow at his side in the dark. Hedi hated always being left behind, but she didn't have a choice right now.

The minutes ticked by slowly. She kept checking her watch, wondering how long to give him. He'd said five minutes, but five minutes was not very long.

At the five-minute mark, she started counting mentally, making it go to six minutes, seven minutes. At the eight-minute mark, she stood, leaning against the tree. She hadn't heard anything, not a gunshot, not a crackle of a branch.

And then suddenly he was right there beside her. Salem shoved her nose into her hand. Hedi stroked and scratched the beautiful animal's neck and chin. She watched as Pierce dropped a heavy load to the ground at her feet. She could hear his heavy gasping breath now that he allowed himself to let it go. His load took the shape of a large prone male. "Which twin is it?"

"Billy. He was moving a little slower than the others, but now he won't do anything until at least morning."

"What about his weapons?"

"I stashed them back there. I want to pick off one more person," he said. "Two against two are the odds I'm looking for."

She smiled, realizing he was at least counting her as an equal, and that made her feel good. "Let me come with you," she said, "then we don't have to ditch the weapons."

He hesitated, then gave a curt nod. "Just remember," he said, "that I spent a lot of time learning how to do this."

She nodded. "And you do it damn well," she said. "But time is definitely of the essence."

He nodded once and whispered, "Come on," and he melted into the darkness.

She was amazed at how soundlessly he moved, with Salem always at his side, as if they were back in the war. And essentially they were. The two were a pair. Was Salem's relationship with Pete like that too?

Was the war ever over for these men?

It seemed to her that every step she made came with a crackle and a crunch. She kept trying to not focus on it, but it was hard because Pierce apparently moved effortlessly and silently.

Suddenly they came up against the side of the house, and she saw Jed, heard him talking. She whispered, "Can you tell if someone is with him?"

"That's Jed, but is he talking to someone on the phone? I don't see anyone else."

Off to their left was a whispered "There you are." And a rifle barrel was locked and loaded with a *clink*.

Pierce wasted no time, taking three steps and diving low. She watched as he flattened the gunman to the ground, pulling the rifle from his hands, then he turned and smacked him hard in the head with the rifle butt. Salem latched onto the stranger's ankle, growling in a most horrible way.

"Easy, girl. We got him."

Slowly he persuaded Salem to back away from the man.

Hedi stood at Pierce's side, taking the rifle as he handed it over to her. "Is that Bobby?" she asked.

"Yeah," he said. "Let's get him to his brother." He looked at her. "Can you grab his feet?"

"I can for a little way," she said, "but these guys …"

"I know," he said. "I carried his brother. Maybe we'll drag him over there and tie him up."

And that was what they did. Back at the house, Salem standing between the two of them, Hedi handed Pierce the rifle and said, "I'd prefer to have a handgun any day."

"As long as I have a weapon, I don't care. Come on. Let's go," he said, running to the corner of the house. In the distance she thought she could hear vehicles. And then Pierce surprised her. He stepped forward, around the corner and said, "Hello, Jed." He raised the confiscated rifle, aiming for Jed's chest.

Jed turned on him, pointed his rifle in Pierce's direction and said, "Don't you fucking come any closer."

"I don't need to," Pierce said gently.

Hedi watched as Salem kept to the shadows behind her around the corner.

"I can shoot you easily from here," Pierce continued. "The fact of the matter is, I want you to get the hell off Pete's property and to leave him and his property alone."

"I don't give a fuck what you want," Jed said, "because I didn't come alone." In one hand he held his rifle, still pointed at Pierce, but, in the other hand, a well-bandaged hand, he held the propane torch. "I came prepared too. I'll burn this place to the ground."

"I can't let you do that," Hedi said, stepping out to join Pierce. "Definitely not happening." She searched the area for a second man but saw no sign of him.

All of a sudden a gun poked her in the back. "Hate to do this," Ross said, "but hands up, Hedi."

"Shit," she said, slurring the word, slowly raising her hands.

"You too, cowboy."

Pierce had absolutely no problem doing the same.

"See?" taunted Jed. "Not alone."

Ross chuckled. "Not such a smartass when a gun's pointed at you, are you, Pierce?"

"I'm enjoying the entertainment here. Thanks, Ross," Jed said, his rifle lowered to his side now, but a wild-eyed expression overtook his face, topped off by a madman's smile.

Hedi turned to look at Ross. "I'm really sorry you did that, Ross."

"I thought about it for a long time, and I figured I was running away with my tail between my legs and with nothing to show for it. Whereas, if I stayed here, I still could get it all," he said calmly.

She nodded gravely, then smiled. "But you're wrong." And she dropped, kicked out, hit him hard in his kneecap. When he buckled, she flipped, kicked him in the jaw, and down he went. She grabbed his rifle and turned, holding it on Jed.

Drunk Jed was a little slow to react—or more entertained with Hedi taking down Ross—and was caught off guard, his rifle still at his side, still pointing downward.

Pierce looked at her, then at Ross groaning on the ground and said, "Wow, nice job."

"Aikido," she said. "Ross, you should have left. But don't you worry. Now you'll for sure get free room and board again but also an awful lot of very unwelcome company."

WITH ROSS AND both Bobby and Billy taken down, that left just Jed. And, hearing the vehicles in the distance, Pierce stepped forward and said, "Jed, put down your firearm and the torch."

"Hell no," Jed snapped. "This ends here and now."

"Absolutely it does," Pierce said quietly. "Your three backups can't help you now. It's just you."

"I didn't need them anyway," he roared. And he raised his firearm.

But, instead of firing, he lit the torch. Pierce swore, took aim and said, "Put that out, or I'll shoot you down."

Without warning, Jed fired but, because of his bad hand, missed. Pierce bolted to the side and dashed behind his truck as Jed laughed like a loon. He'd obviously flipped a mental switch and was incapable of rational action or thought.

Realizing Hedi was behind him, they split and came up on either side of Jed. But he was already lighting bits of grass with the torch as he moved toward the house, laughing more and more. Flames licked up the dry overgrown grass, racing in all directions.

At the front veranda Jed howled, "You can't stop me," he said. "Even if you shoot me, I'll drop this, and it'll light up this place like nothing."

"We'll put it out before it gets anywhere," Pierce said calmly. "We have to redo that deck out back and put in a ramp anyway, just like for this veranda."

"No fucking way Pete's coming home," Jed said. "This is Ross's place, and he doesn't want no broken-person ramp." He turned the torch toward the steps.

Pierce jumped him, knocking away the rifle, but Jed sent blue flames at him. Pierce jumped back, and Jed, realizing his advantage, started to laugh again.

"Come and get me," he jeered. "You think I don't want to toast your skin alive for what you did to my hand?"

The vehicle din got louder. "This won't end well," Pierce said. He used hand signals to keep Salem behind him. If Jed saw her, he'd make her his first target. She deserved better than that. He called out to Jed, "The cops are coming. Everybody in town and even from neighboring counties who can give us a hand are headed here. You sure you want to take a bullet and die this way?"

"Why the fuck not? At least I'll see this place burn. You took away my wife and kids. You blew up my hand. You ruined my life."

"Oh, grow up," Hedi snapped beside him. "You're the one who chased away your wife and kids. You're the one who ruined your life. And no way in hell we'll let you just stand here and burn down Pete's place."

"Well, Pete ain't coming back," he snapped. "So shut the fuck up."

"Jed?" A thin but valiant voice called from the first vehicle to come up the driveway. Even in the dark the voice was recognizable. "What the hell are you doing, man?"

Pierce barely caught Salem as she went to race past him. Giving her a hard command to wait, she sat but squirmed in eagerness. She'd had no trouble recognizing Pete's voice. But the danger wasn't over. Jed had a personal hatred for the dog …

Jed faltered. He turned to the pickup parked sideways in the drive.

Pete opened the door so everybody could see him. Jessie hopped out of the driver's side, came around to Pete, dropped his wheelchair down on the ground and helped him into it.

Pierce and Hedi exchanged a glance, both wondering how Pete got here and ended up in Jessie's vehicle.

Jed's face worked up into a big frown. "What the hell? Ross said you weren't coming back."

"Would you shut that torch off please?" Pete said quietly. "You'll burn down my house, and I need it."

"You should have stayed where you were," Jed said, moving a couple steps closer. He held the torch out in front of him, as if to burn Pete. "We don't need no broken-down pieces of sorry-ass shits here."

Pete nodded. "You know what? Ross told me that too. Not in the same words but basically telling me this was a place for only able-bodied men, and everybody else needed to stay in the rehab center. And I'm sorry to say I believed him. My belief in myself had taken so many hits already that I allowed his words to dictate my actions." He turned to look at Pierce and smiled. "Pierce here reminded me that I've been through worse and probably there'll be worse ahead of me too. But you don't need to be worried about that anymore. They'll lock you up for a long time."

"Why? I haven't done nothing," Jed said, laughing uproariously. "So what if I got a blowtorch? Big fucking deal." He turned it on the grass and lit the grass around him on fire.

Pierce watched him, wondering if Jed realized how close

he was to torching his own body. "Is that how you want to die?" he asked softly. "Do you want to burn yourself alive?"

"What do you care?"

Pierce crossed his arms over his chest. "I don't. I've seen too many people light themselves on fire over in Afghanistan and India. It's not a pretty sight. But, if that's your way to go, well, whatever, man."

"I'm not suicidal," Jed roared. "It's you who'll burn alive."

Pierce just stared at him. "I don't think so. You're the one looking pretty weak and feeble at the moment."

Jed looked around, as if seeing the ten men surrounding him for the first time. He frowned. "Who the fuck are you guys?"

"Law-abiding citizens and cops from Fort Collins," the closest police officer said. "We sure as hell aren't in our usual jurisdiction, but, if we got to step in, we got to. And you're causing trouble. Where the hell your local sheriff is, I don't know."

"He's sitting in his office, not worrying about jack shit," Jed said. "That's the way he likes it."

"Maybe," the cop said, "but that's not his job." He turned, caught sight of Hedi and nodded. "So we got one deputy, and that's it?"

"Yeah, nobody else would come," she said. "And I've been fired because I did come."

The cop raised his eyebrows. "I'm pretty sure there'll be an investigation."

"Maybe," she said. "Doesn't mean it'll make any difference. Apparently our sheriff paid everybody to vote him in."

"Wow. That'll make for some fun times coming up." The police officer looked at Jed. "You going to put that out and drop your weapon?"

"Hell no," Jed said. "You want me to do that, you'll have to shoot me."

"I can," the cop said in a bored tone of voice. "It's your choice." He pointed his revolver at Jed. "Make a decision."

"Absolutely," Jed said, and he turned on Pierce with the blowtorch and jumped him.

Shots broke out, but Jed was too close to Pierce for a good rifle shot. Jed went down, shot in the shoulder, but still fighting mad. He threw himself at Pierce.

Pierce sidestepped the man, grabbed the blowtorch from his hand, shut it off, stopping the blue flame, and stomped out the grass fire Jed had started.

Jed swore and cussed, and, as they watched, then dropped to the ground, crying like a baby.

Hedi threw herself into Pierce's arms.

He held her close and said, "It's okay. It's over."

She gave him a quick hug, looked up at him and said, "It might be over, but you damn near got torched."

"Maybe," he said, "but Jed was a little too drunk for that."

Jed was quickly secured, medical aid administered. The rest of the prisoners were taken out, and explanations were given.

Pierce didn't know how many men were here from Fort Collins, how many were locals. Or why Salem disappeared. He'd figured for sure she'd have gone right for Pete but ... He glanced around, his gaze searching the area. She'd had a rough time of it lately; so, if this many men scared her off, that was fine. She could have a private reunion with Pete a little later.

As he looked over the crowd, he found Jessie and Pete.

He walked over, squatting in front of Pete, and said, "Man, you're a sight for sore eyes."

Pete reached out to shake his hand. "Thank you. And I don't mean for saving the house. Obviously that's just property. But thank you for not taking any more lives. This isn't the war we're supposed to fight, and we're never supposed to fight one on our own soil."

Pierce understood exactly what he meant. "I hear you," he said. "I figured we could probably make some rough house renos, if you want to move in tonight, and then we'll get to work over the next couple weeks to get this place fixed up for you."

He watched as Pete's jawline worked, trying to hold back his emotions.

Hedi reached over and said, "Hey, Pete, it's so good to see you." She opened her arms and gave him a hug.

Pete clasped his arms around her and just held her tight. "You got a good guy here," he said. "Make sure you don't lose him."

"He's not mine to lose," Hedi said with a laugh. "Why would you think that?"

"That's just the way it looks on the outside," her dad said. "Honestly, I'm delighted you lost the boyfriends you did. They should stay lost too. But I agree. This one's a keeper."

Pierce snorted at that. "I'm glad y'all approve, but we got to get some people back in this house. I'm sure Pete would like to go in and take a look."

"He would," Pete said. "But there's one other thing I really want to know."

Pierce nodded. Pete wondered where Salem was. Only Pierce had no idea where Salem had snuck away to.

Just then a kerfuffle was heard at the trucks. Jed had somehow managed to get another firearm free and was holding a handgun against a cop's neck. "You guys are going to let me go," Jed yelled, anger now replacing the tears from earlier. "No fucking way I'm going to jail for the rest of my life."

"Maybe not if you're dead," Pierce said.

Backing up, dragging the cop with him, Jed said, "If you think I won't kill this guy, you're wrong."

"You might shoot him," one of the other officers said, "but you'll get a dozen bullets yourself. You won't survive."

Jed kept backing up toward the barn where his truck was. "Maybe. Or you guys can let me go. I'll take off out of here, and you'll never see me again."

Pierce didn't believe that, and he sure as hell wasn't interested in making a deal with a drunk lunatic. But Pierce caught something out of the corner of his eye and realized another element had joined the fray, looking for a revenge of her own. She hadn't snuck away. Salem had snuck *around*. Still caught up in a war not of her making, she'd kept her eye on the enemy, even when the others had relaxed.

Pierce swore gently under his breath. This wouldn't be good.

Pete asked, "What's the matter?"

"There'll be bloodshed," Pierce said. "I just don't know how severe it'll be."

"It's already pretty damn bad," Hedi said. "So, if you've got a way to save that cop, I don't really give a shit about Jed."

Pierce nodded. "The trouble is, somebody has already got her own plan of action. On a target she can't see past."

Pete's breath sucked in hard. "Salem? Are you talking

about Salem?"

"I think so," Pierce said. He bolted off to the side.

Jed roared, "Get your ass back here."

Jed fired in Pierce's direction, but Pierce was already out of range and hiding behind the closest vehicle. Where he was, he could see Salem. It was the hidden element they needed, but it would be damn hard to stop her from killing Jed. She shifted, and Pierce lost sight of her. Frantic, he peered around the edge of the vehicle looking for her. Suddenly a harsh growl came, and the dog shot through the air and attached itself to Jed's shoulder.

Jed screamed. The gun went off harmlessly into the air as the dog ripped him backward, flat onto the ground. She released her grip and came in at another angle, looking for his throat. Jed screamed and rolled his arms over his head, trying to protect himself.

Pierce raced forward and kicked the gun out of Jed's hand as the cop backed away.

"Salem," Pierce cried out. "Stop."

Salem growled harder.

"Good girl," Pierce said. "We got him, and you're right. He was going to hurt this man. Good girl."

The growling eased slightly, but the dog didn't let go of Jed. Salem was obviously confused and unsure.

Pete in his wheelchair, struggling in the rough ground, came up behind Pierce. "Salem?" he asked, his voice almost broken.

Salem's ears pointed skyward. Her gaze lifted until she caught sight of Pete.

Pierce watched as recognition slammed into her. She released Jed from her jaws and bounded forward. And into Pete's lap, almost knocking him and the wheelchair over.

Pete wrapped his arms around her, his tears evident.

He hugged the dog tight. "Oh, my God. Salem!"

The cops had Jed under guard now. Pierce looked at them. "Do you think you can keep him this time?"

The man, grim faced, nodded. "He's a slippery bugger."

They handcuffed Jed, ignoring the screams as his shoulder was wrenched backward into the steel bracelets.

"He'll need medical treatment," one of the cops said, "though I'd just as soon put a bullet in his head than do that."

"If he has an accident on the way to the hospital, I won't complain," Pierce said. He looked at Jed with a hard glance. "If you ever come back on this property, you can bet there's a bullet that'll hit you right here." He poked Jed between the eyes. "So you're warned."

But Jed was in too much pain to bluster. Instead he blubbered like a child. The alcoholic haze was dimming, and the reality was setting in.

"On top of that," Pierce said, "your property now belongs to your wife and the kids. You will not fight it. Do you hear me?"

Jed glared at him. "Or what?"

"Or else …" Pierce snapped, "I won't be leaving Pete alone for a while. I will make sure your wife and kids get what they deserve too. You'll go to jail for a hell of a long time. Don't be such an asshole as to take a roof away from over their heads."

Jed's gaze dropped to his feet. "I won't fight it," he muttered. "She won't stick around for me anyway, for when I come out of jail."

"Why would she?" Hedi said. "You beat her. You beat the kids. You terrorized them all."

Jed appeared to crumble in front of everyone. "I took a wrong step somewhere," he said. "And I couldn't find my way back."

"Now you have lots of time to think about your return journey," Hedi snapped. She stepped back, glancing at her father. "Thanks for bringing Pete."

"I didn't," he said. He pointed at one of the other strangers. "This guy works at the rehab center. At Pete's behest, he brought him down. We intercepted him on the road, and I brought Pete here myself. I figured that, if I came in, Jed would let me get close enough to drop Pete off. And that might be enough to defuse the situation."

"Maybe," she said. "But it was really Salem who put an end to it."

Pierce turned back to Pete. Salem had barely calmed down her excitement at seeing him again. She kept licking his face, trying to climb into his lap. And Pete looked like a new man. Pierce reached down, scratching Salem's forehead. She leaned into his hand, one of the happiest-looking dogs he'd ever seen. He crouched beside the two of them. "I sure hope you'll stay here now, Pete, because this girl needs you."

Pete nodded. "Like Jed will find out, it was a hard journey back, but I'm here now. And I won't leave her again." He looked at Pierce. "Are you serious about helping out?"

Pierce nodded. "I don't have a job, don't really have a home at the moment. I can go back to New Mexico and pick up my life there, but I'm more than willing to give you a hand for a couple weeks to get this house modified so it can be yours in all ways again."

Pete nodded. "I'd really appreciate it. I still have to get the accounting sorted through, but I think enough money is there to do some of the modifications."

They looked up as Hedi approached.

Pete frowned at her. "Is it true you got fired?"

She nodded, shoving her hands in her pockets. "And maybe that's a good thing," she admitted. "As you know, I can swing a hammer. If Pierce knows what to do here to update your home, then I can be a sidekick and give him an extra pair of working hands."

Several men stepped forward, and one was a spokesman for all. "We can help too. Some of us are working but have time on weekends. If we'd known that's all that was needed, we would have been here a long time ago. We're sorry, Pete."

More tears came to Pete's eyes. He brushed them away impatiently. "I can't tell you how much I appreciate this."

"We get it," Pierce said. "Or maybe they don't understand it, but I do. Because I've been there. And I know how important it is to have people help you make this last transition." He looked around the yard, seeing the cop vehicles backing out. He walked to where Jessie was. "What about the sheriff?"

"He's being relieved of his duties as we speak," Jessie said. "We're looking for someone to step in as interim sheriff, and we'll hold elections as soon as we can. It's not a job I care to do anymore." Jessie looked at Pierce, crossing his arms over his chest. "What about you? You could try it—for the interim. Then let the people decide. Why don't you sign up to be sheriff?"

Pierce's jaw dropped. When he recovered, he gave a broken laugh. "Because I'd shoot guys like Jed."

"But ... because you didn't, even when he gave you lots of opportunities, means you're the right man for the job," Jessie said shrewdly.

Several of the men in the group stepped up behind him

and nodded. "You'd make a great sheriff," several of them said.

"I don't have enough money to pay people in this town to vote me in," Pierce said in disgust. "And, if that's what they want, they sure as hell don't want me because I'm not the kind of guy to turn my eye when there's cheating, lying, stealing, breaking and entering, arson and murder, not to mention making moonshine. And any person who'll abuse an animal on my watch just might feel the lash of my belt."

Jessie nodded. "Like I said, you'd make a great sheriff. We can't have you taking your belt to anyone, but just knowing you're around will kick some ass. It'll stop most people from crossing that line."

As Pierce frowned, Hedi slipped her hand into the crook of his elbow. "And, no, I didn't put them up to it. It was my dad's idea. I'd already mentioned it to you. I think you'd be a hell of a sheriff."

At that, Pierce snorted. "You don't know me very well."

"I know you well enough," she said. "And I'm hoping to get to know you better. Either way, I still think you're the right person for the town."

He looked down at her and shrugged. "I doubt anybody would elect me. I'm a stranger. The population seems to want your current sheriff, or they want your dad. I'm nobody."

"Not true," said one of the men behind Jessie. "This has already been preapproved by the townsfolk in an emergency Town Hall meeting tonight. You'll find you get more support than you expect."

"Well then, we'll see," Pierce said, tilting his head, giving a short nod. "I guess you can put my name on the ballot. Doesn't mean I'll get the job though."

Hedi and Jessie exchanged a glance that made Pierce suspicious. But their smiles were obvious.

"You guys really think I'd win?"

"Hell yeah," Jessie said. He smacked Pierce hard on the shoulder. "Welcome to town. You're already hired as the interim sheriff. Election in three months. Of course we have to get that paperwork in order." He stopped and chuckled. "Maybe I should make that *Welcome to the family*." He turned, still laughing uproariously, and walked back to his truck.

Within a few minutes, all the vehicles disappeared down the road, leaving Pierce, Hedi, Salem and Pete in the yard.

Pete looked from one to the other. "Is it that serious?"

Pierce looked at Hedi, wrapped an arm around her shoulders, tucking her close. "We haven't had two seconds to know the answer to that. I know which way I'm leaning, but I hate to rush a lady."

She chuckled. "All you've done is rush me." She reached up, kissing him on the cheek. "Let's just say, Pete, we're both looking to finding out if my dad's right."

Pete smiled, his arms looped around Salem, who looked like she'd finally found her home again. "So what's the chance some food is in the house? I'm hungry."

Salem barked in agreement.

And, on that note, everyone laughed. They headed inside to see how much of the groceries Hedi had brought they could eat right now.

CHAPTER 14

H EDI LEARNED MORE about house renovations than she thought possible. Pierce himself appeared to be always around, always helping, always building, regardless of the work being done. And, sure enough, with Hedi at his side, her father and several other volunteers had gutted the bathroom and were even now installing grab bars for Pete to use.

Tiling was about to start, and that was the finishing stage. The en suite bathroom was completely open so Pete could get a wheelchair in and out, or he could walk on his prosthetics, with or without crutches. So far the prosthetics offered to Peter were pretty ugly in appearance and fit and definitely in need of an upgrade, but a phone call from Kat, Badger's partner, had given Pete the best news ever. She was willing to take him on to get him something more advanced and which would serve him well.

Pete still had both arms, but one had been injured and was weaker. He could use it to pick up a cup and a knife and a fork, but he wasn't capable of doing much work with it. But Pierce had already devised a set of weights that would help Pete strengthen those muscles. Hedi had helped as much as she could, swinging a hammer, pounding nails, making coffee and even cooking meals, if making sandwiches counted.

Two days later her dad showed up midafternoon and told Pierce, "You've got about four days to finish up here, son. Then your days will be full."

Pierce, sitting with a cup of coffee beside Pete, looked at Jessie and said, "I need more than four days to finish this rehab, so what are you talking about?"

"This." Jessie handed over a piece of paper. Pierce looked at it, and his jaw dropped.

Hedi had some inkling of what it was because she'd heard her father and his buddies talking about it.

She herself had been reinstated to her position but had taken the week off to help out Pete and Pierce. She couldn't afford more time off now that Stephen and Roy had both been removed from office. Even the dispatcher had been replaced. A lot of court cases would be filed soon, charging the sheriff with various crimes, although she wasn't exactly sure with what. Ross, the Billy boys, and Jed wouldn't be seeing daylight for a long time. She wanted to feel sorry for them but couldn't. They were assholes of the first order. Pierce handed the piece of paper to her, and she could see the stunned look on his face.

But Pete had been looking at the page over Pierce's shoulder, and he started to laugh. He reached out and smacked Pierce on the shoulder. "Well, Interim Sheriff, how do you feel?"

Pierce shook his head. "I told you that I'm probably not any good at this," he warned.

"And I told you that we need somebody who can make decisions on the side of right," her father said quietly. "You've got three months to prove you're the right man for the job." He grinned. "I've asked to be on the committee for the election, and you can bet I'll be doing a lot of lobbying to get you in there. The town was pretty fed up with the old sheriff." He looked around at the renovations and said, "I love this. Nice job."

"So then what? You'll take over my spot here?" Pierce asked jokingly.

"Nope, you've got the rest of this week. You're supposed to show up for work on Monday," he said. "If we absolutely have to, we can push that back a week, but, considering nobody is in the station, we need you as soon as possible."

"Understood," Pierce said, frowning.

Hedi could see the wheels turning in his head. Apparently her father could too. "Think out loud, son. Think out loud," Jessie said. "We can't figure out what you're considering until you speak up."

"I'm thinking about how much work there is to be done here," he said slowly. "I don't want to leave Pete in the lurch."

"I was kind of hoping you'd live here for a bit," Pete said. "Even as the sheriff, you can stay here."

Pierce looked at him in surprise. "Are you okay with that?"

Pete grinned. "Hell yes. I'd like to see you live here for a long time, but that would entail Hedi moving in too, and I highly doubt she wants that," Pete teased.

Hedi could feel the color washing up her cheeks. "That's not fair," she said.

Her father guffawed loudly. "You're in a shitty-ass little rental now. What you guys should do is fix up someplace nearby, so you're close to Pete."

"That won't happen anytime soon," Pierce said calmly. "Pete's renos are the first priority. We have to make sure he's got a fully accessible kitchen and bathroom and properly equipped vehicle and that he can get in and out of his house on his own. We can work on the rest afterward."

"The rest?" Pete said, dazed. "What else could you possibly do?"

"Depends if you want access to the upstairs or not," Pierce said. "We could put in an elevator."

Pete looked at him, and his jaw dropped. "That would be a lot of money."

"It would be some money," Pierce said with a nod. "So that's one of those questions where you have to ask, is it worth it to you?"

"Wow." Pete looked at Pierce and said, "But you still haven't answered me."

"I guess it's a yes then," Pierce said, "but, about starting the job as sheriff, I want to make sure that bathroom is 100 percent ready and that we've opened up those double front doors and I've at least gutted this kitchen."

Pete just chuckled. "You know that usually these renos take months, right?"

Pierce shrugged and said, "For a lot of people it takes months. But for a lot of people it doesn't. I promised you full accessibility, and I'll make sure you get it."

"We'll keep working," Jessie said. "Once you're sheriff, you can be in a supervisory capacity here. Come home after work and tell us what to do the next day."

Pete clapped his hands and shouted with joy. "I can't believe this," he said. "Why the hell didn't I come home earlier?"

"Because Pierce wasn't here," Hedi said. "Remember that part."

Pete gripped Pierce's wrist. "Man, I owe you big-time."

Pierce shook his head. "We all owe you," he said firmly.

"You took a hit for our country."

Pete mumbled under his breath and then said, "I sure wish the rest of the world thought the way you do."

"You have a good group of friends around you now," Pierce said, all the others nodding. "You should be fine."

Pete looked at Pierce and asked, "And what about you? You'll accept the help being offered too?"

"What help? I don't need any help." Pierce frowned.

Hedi heard a vehicle came up the road and chuckled. She knew exactly who was coming. What she didn't know was how Pete would respond to the upcoming news.

Just then her father decided it was time to go. "Pierce, date?"

He sighed. "A week from Monday," he said. "I'd like the extra week off to make sure Pete's okay."

"I'll go in next week, Dad," Hedi said.

"Good enough. A lot of people went to bat for you, Pierce. We know you'll do a good job." And, on that note, he turned, and his cronies walked out with him.

It was already late in the afternoon, almost dinnertime. Hedi looked at Pete and Pierce and said, "Barbecued steaks for dinner?"

"I would absolutely love a barbecued steak," Pete said. "Used to love barbecuing." He looked at his prosthetics and frowned.

"Today sounds like a great day to get back into it," Pierce said. "We'll move the grill up on the deck, so you can get to it."

Pete grinned. "Wouldn't that be something?"

"Remember that your legs are injured, not your hands," Hedi said, as she'd said many times before. There seemed to be this disconnect sometimes with Pete because, being without his lower legs, he had a sense of not being able to do anything. Whereas he was capable of doing so much more. She'd even caught him swinging a hammer today with Pierce. A little weak and off center but he was helping and smiling as he did so. She smiled. "I'll take Pierce out for a walk, if you don't mind."

"Absolutely not," Pete said, waving at the backyard and beyond, grinning. "You guys need private time too. When are you moving in, Hedi?"

She shot him a look and shook her head.

He nodded. "Pierce will be living here for a while," he said. "At least I hope."

"I won't leave you in the lurch," Pierce said. "Doesn't mean somebody else might want to take my place though."

Just then a knock came at the door. Pete called out, "The door's unlocked. Come on in."

The door pushed open, followed by light footsteps. Then a soft female voice. "Pete?"

Hedi watched the color drain from Pete's face. He shook his head and said, "No. Oh, hell no."

In a firm voice Hedi said, "Yes."

He looked at her, startled.

"You are *not* disabled," she said. "You're perfectly capable of handling anything and everything life throws at you. You need to gain some strength. You need to have a mindset shift. But you're well on the way. And that means you can shift in all directions."

And just then a beautiful blonde walked into the kitchen with her eyes locked on Pete. Her gaze went to his shorts and the prosthetics on his lower legs. She swallowed hard and then looked up at him and said, "Why didn't you call me?"

Pete's jaw dropped, and he tried to answer her. He

looked at Hedi and Pierce for help.

Hedi grabbed Pierce's hand and said, "Glad you came, Lina. Pete's having second thoughts, *wiser* thoughts, about life now, and he's doing so much better. It's a perfect time for you to come and say hi to him." As she stepped outside, she said, "We'll leave you two alone to talk. We're barbe-quing steaks later. You're welcome to stay."

Lina looked at her and said, "I don't understand."

"Pete was trying to be the brave warrior and to let you live your life without him holding you back," she said.

A flush of anger washed over Lina's face, and she round-ed on Pete. "Did you think my love was so superficial?"

Hedi and Pierce, still holding hands, dashed out the back door in the kitchen, hearing raised voices even as they continued across the backyard. And then, all of a sudden, there was silence. Pierce glanced at her and said, "That was pretty devious."

"Men like to caterwaul a lot," she said quietly. "And Pete will make a big deal out of meeting her again and about his injuries. It wasn't necessary. Pete's so much more capable than he thought."

"A lot of it is mind-set," Pierce said. "Pete mentioned her once."

"Good," she said shortly. "Pete broke Lina's heart. May-be now they can work it out."

"So you're a little bit of a matchmaker, are you?" He wrapped his arms around her shoulders and tucked her close.

She chuckled and said, "Maybe. It's been really nice to have you around these last few days, without all the craziness when we first met."

She walked to a spot in the meadow where beautiful mossy grass grew under one of the big trees, and the stream trickled past close by. She sat down and patted the grass beside her. "Let's just sit a while and give them a chance to relax."

"I'm all for it." He lay down with his knees bent, staring up at the sky. "Did you bring me here for a reason?"

She shot him a look. "Maybe."

She hopped up, and he twisted to see her pull a blanket out from the boughs of the tree branches and spread it out. He moved onto it and opened his arms. She dropped to the ground and sagged against his chest. "There is just something about matchmaking," she said, "that makes you want a little something extra special for yourself."

He tilted her chin up and kissed her. "I meant everything I've said so far. I really don't want to lose you." He kissed her again and again. "Lina?"

"Well, Lina is a very determined woman," she said. "I wouldn't be at all surprised if she doesn't stay tonight."

Pierce's eyebrows shot up.

She nodded. "So you might be the one wanting to move out a little earlier than you thought."

"I've been wondering about staying at your place for a long time. You've never taken me there. I figured maybe it was out of bounds."

"Not at all. But it's not all that nice," she said. "And it's not big enough for two of us."

"You've brought your dog once or twice, but that's it. I have yet to meet the cat."

"My thought was maybe eventually we could move into a house together. One for both of us."

He nodded slowly. "I'd like that. I'd love to build us one. But not yet," he said slowly, holding her against his chest and gently stroking his fingers through her hair. "Not only do we have Pete to get back on his feet, but Vicky and the kids' house needs work."

"I'm sure you'll recruit the exact same guys to help out."

"Yep. I don't think there will be a problem with that," he said comfortably. "But I'm not sure there's any money for those renos."

"We can do some fund-raising for her," Hedi said, snuggling in deeper.

"You're good people, you know that?" he whispered, kissing her on the forehead.

"You're good people too," she said, chuckling. She leaned up on her elbow, rolled over on his chest again and kissed him. "We don't have much time," she whispered, dropping him another kiss. And then another one.

She sat up, straddling him and slowly pulled her T-shirt up and over her head. His hands slid up to her ribs, cupping her bra-covered breasts and murmuring, "I'm not sure there's anything quite as nice as making love outside."

She nodded. "I figured you would think so. It's not that I'm into public displays," she said, "but there's something so very elemental about being out under the wind and the sun, just the two of us." Then a bird flew over, squawking at them. She chuckled. "And Mother Nature."

Before she realized it, her bra slid down her arms. She watched the look of wonder come over his face, and she'd never felt more beautiful as she sat on his hips. "In theory," she said, "what we're doing is pretty perfect, but we still have on way-too-many clothes."

He chuckled. She straightened, stood and stepped to the side, where she kicked off her sandals and shimmied out of her jeans. There she stood in just a tiny scrap of lace and cocked an eye at him. "Like what you see?" she challenged.

He bolted to his feet, his T-shirt going in one direction, his shoes in another, and his jeans and briefs hitting the ground faster than she thought possible. And then he stood before her, his eyes feasting on her, and she chuckled.

His gaze ripped up to hers, and he asked, "What's so amusing?"

She pointed at his feet. "You still have a sock on."

He pulled it off and then pointed at the scrap of lace she still wore. "You still have clothes on too."

She took a step closer and said, "You do it."

He snatched her up into his arms and kissed her with a hot fierce passion that ignited a storm between the two of them. He'd wanted this right from the beginning, but, with everything else going on, there just hadn't been that perfect moment to explore each other. She wrapped her arms tight around his neck and half climbed his frame. Finally he picked her up, his hands under her buttocks and lifted her so he completely held her. She gasped and said, "What about your prosthetic?"

"Do you hear me complaining?" he whispered and kissed her passionately.

Finally she couldn't stand it anymore. She slid her legs back down, dropped herself to the blanket and opened her arms. He kneeled beside her, pulled off the scrap of lace and let his eyes feast on the bounty before him. He stroked her legs from her toes, over her knees and upper thighs, to gently curl in the tiny strip of hair between her legs. She moaned as his fingers delved gently between the plump folds and then slowly moved up to caress her hip bones. He spread apart her legs, with his knees planted between them, dropped a kiss right at the tip of the tiny strip of hair and dragged his lips to her belly button, where he dotted a line of kisses to one hip and then the other. His fingers were stroking, caressing, sliding under, separating her cheeks, touching spots she hadn't realized were so sensitive. She arched and moved, shifting forward and backward from his touch and then needing so much more of it. She grabbed handfuls of his hair and pulled him up, closer to her face. She whispered, "Come. I want you now."

But he resisted her orders, letting his fingers stoke the fire as he gently, reverently explored her body—the hills, the dips, the smooth skin along her ribs and over her hips. Slowly he stroked her flat belly to slide through the curls at the apex of her legs.

"Pierce," she cried out, her fingers clenching and releasing as she twisted beneath his ministrations.

"*Shhh*, I'm here," he whispered, sliding a finger between the moist skin folds to slide one finger in and then two …

She moaned, twisting her hips, rising and falling in response to the rhythm of his fingers. She reared up, tugged on his upper arms and pulled him toward her, ordering, "Come."

Chuckling, he shifted closer, supporting his weight on his elbows. He positioned his hips so he slid just inside her and stopped. He leaned over, taking her lips in a rousing kiss, his tongue sliding deep inside to war with hers. At the same time he slowly penetrated her body.

She moaned, her hips wiggling, adjusting to his unexpected size. And finally he was there, seated at the heart of her. When she could, she opened her eyes to stare up at him and whispered, "It feels so damn good."

He nodded, his voice harsh and deep, as he whispered, "Yes. But only because it's you." He kissed her again and again, but he kept his body still.

She twisted against him, her hips trying to rise up to set him in motion, but he wasn't having any of it. Finally she lay still, her body acquiescing as he slowly pulled back and then dove in again and again and again. She cried out, her body now writhing beneath him as she arched. He drove deeper and deeper, longer and harder, until finally she exploded, crying out for him.

He held her close in his arms as he drove in again and again until his body shuddered, quaking in his own release. A moment later he slowly rolled over on his side and tucked her close to him. Together, with the afternoon sun beating down on their heated bodies, they slowly recovered.

"Wow," she whispered moments later.

He nodded but didn't seem too bothered about talking.

She grinned, reached to kiss him and said, "Not into small talk, are you?"

"You did me in," he said, his voice still hoarse.

"Does that mean you're done for now then?"

His eyes flew open. "Hell no." He kissed her lightly. "We have just gotten started." He grinned and hugged her close.

"Promise?" she whispered.

He gazed deeply into her eyes and answered, "I promise."

EPILOGUE

E VEN AS PIERCE stared in disbelief as the votes came in—giving him the job of the sheriff in Arrowhead, Colorado—back in New Mexico, Zane Carmichael sat down at Badger's desk and said, "I hear some dog hunting is going on."

Badger shifted back in his chair, steepled his fingers and studied Zane. "Do you have any K9 experience?"

"No," he said. "Artillery IEDs, all kinds of military experience, but nothing with dogs. On the other hand, I was raised with them, and I'd say I have a talent for them."

Badger's eyebrows pulled together. "Tell me more."

"Animals of all kinds speak to me," he said. "It's just easier for me than for a lot of people. I've had basic dog obedience training but not the high-level training of K9 handlers."

"Here's what we've got so far," Badger said and spent ten minutes sorting through what they'd done to date.

"I know Ethan and Pierce both had K9 training," Zane said. "I'd like to try though."

"We have ten files," Badger said. "The top of the pack was lost at the airport in Bangor, Maine. His last confirmed location was Stetson, Maine."

"Stetson?" Zane frowned. "How about any other place but there?"

"Why is that?"

"I've got family back in Maine, just outside of Corinna,"

he said. "As much as I love my family, Holly, my younger brother's widow, is somebody I'm trying to avoid."

"Why?" Badger asked.

Zane gave him a lopsided glance. "I cared too much. Brody's widow was my ex-girlfriend. After my baby brother passed away, I went home for the funeral but left as soon as I could. Holly was leaning on me too much, as if wanting me to step into my brother's shoes, and that was the last thing I wanted," Zane said bluntly. "I'd like to be loved for myself, not because I'm a reflection of another man."

"Wow," Badger said. "Sounds like you need to get back to Maine then." He picked up the file. "I've got a younger male here called Katch." He frowned at the name. "He's well-known for his ability to catch apparently." He studied the first page. "He was sent home after not following commands well enough under fire. He ended up with PTSD after one particularly bad bombing, and they couldn't get him to function properly afterward. He was returned to a training compound, then shipped out to an adopted family. He was lost at the airport, and the adopted family never got him. He showed up in Bangor, and we were alerted, but nobody could catch him. Our last notification said he was picked up by a hunter. Considering Katch is suffering from PTSD, that could be problematic. Now we're not sure where he is. Last known sighting was Stetson."

"Dammit." Zane studied the stack of files. "You sure you don't want to give me one of the others—a long way away from Maine?"

"Just for that reason alone," Badger said, leaning forward, "sounds to me like Maine it is. If you're ready ..." He picked up the file and tossed it at him. "Katch."

This concludes Book 2 of The K9 Files: Pierce.
Read about Zane: The K9 Files, Book 3

THE K9 FILES: ZANE (BOOK #3)

Going home wasn't part of his plan ...

Agreeing to travel home to Maine to hunt down Ketch, a K9 dog the system had lost track of, wasn't an easy decision for Zane. It meant facing his drunk of a father, his cold older brother and, worst of all, Angela, his kid brother's widow—who used to be his girlfriend.

Finding Ketch looked to be the easiest part of this dysfunctional homecoming. Only he wasn't the only one hunting Ketch.

Angela has been through a whirlwind of emotions in the last few years. But the good thing in all of this was the hope that Zane would finally come home again. They had a history to clear up and a future to forge ... she hoped.

A call for help brings the injured shepherd to Angela's doorstep, plus a hunter looking to finish what he started. All thoughts of a future with Zane are threatened now and forever as the hunter decides two-legged prey are just as good as four-legged ones.

Book 3 is available now!

To find out more visit Dale Mayer's website.

http://smarturl.it/DMSZane

Author's Note

Thank you for reading Pierce: The K9 Files, Book 2! If you enjoyed the book, please take a moment and leave a short review.

Dear reader,

I love to hear from readers, and you can contact me at my website: www.dalemayer.com or at my Facebook author page. To be informed of new releases and special offers, sign up for my newsletter or follow me on BookBub. And if you are interested in joining Dale Mayer's Reader Group, here is the Facebook sign up page.
facebook.com/groups/402384989872660

Cheers,
Dale Mayer

Get THREE Free Books Now!

Have you met the SEALS of Honor?

SEALs of Honor Books 1, 2, and 3. Follow the stories of brave, badass warriors who serve their country with honor and love their women to the limits of life and death.

Read Mason, Hawk, and Dane right now for FREE.

Go here and tell me where to send them!
http://smarturl.it/EthanBofB

About the Author

Dale Mayer is a USA Today bestselling author best known for her Psychic Visions and Family Blood Ties series. Her contemporary romances are raw and full of passion and emotion (Second Chances, SKIN), her thrillers will keep you guessing (By Death series), and her romantic comedies will keep you giggling (It's a Dog's Life and Charmin Marvin Romantic Comedy series).

She honors the stories that come to her – and some of them are crazy and break all the rules and cross multiple genres!

To go with her fiction, she also writes nonfiction in many different fields with books available on resume writing, companion gardening and the US mortgage system. She has recently published her Career Essentials Series. All her books are available in print and ebook format.

Connect with Dale Mayer Online

Dale's Website – www.dalemayer.com
Twitter – @DaleMayer
Facebook – dalemayer.com/fb
BookBub – bookbub.com/authors/dale-mayer

Also by Dale Mayer

Published Adult Books:

The K9 Files
Ethan, Book 1
Pierce, Book 2
Zane, Book 3

Lovely Lethal Gardens
Arsenic in the Azaleas, Book 1
Bones in the Begonias, Book 2
Corpse in the Carnations, Book 3
Daggers in the Dahlias, Book 4
Evidence in the Echinacea, Book 5
Footprints in the Ferns, Book 6

Psychic Vision Series
Tuesday's Child
Hide 'n Go Seek
Maddy's Floor
Garden of Sorrow
Knock Knock...
Rare Find
Eyes to the Soul
Now You See Her
Shattered
Into the Abyss

Seeds of Malice
Eye of the Falcon
Itsy-Bitsy Spider
Unmasked
Deep Beneath
Psychic Visions Books 1–3
Psychic Visions Books 4–6
Psychic Visions Books 7–9

By Death Series
Touched by Death
Haunted by Death
Chilled by Death
By Death Books 1–3

Broken Protocols – Romantic Comedy Series
Cat's Meow
Cat's Pajamas
Cat's Cradle
Cat's Claus
Broken Protocols 1-4

Broken and... Mending
Skin
Scars
Scales (of Justice)
Broken but... Mending 1-3

Glory
Genesis
Tori
Celeste
Glory Trilogy

Biker Blues

Morgan: Biker Blues, Volume 1
Cash: Biker Blues, Volume 2

SEALs of Honor

Mason: SEALs of Honor, Book 1
Hawk: SEALs of Honor, Book 2
Dane: SEALs of Honor, Book 3
Swede: SEALs of Honor, Book 4
Shadow: SEALs of Honor, Book 5
Cooper: SEALs of Honor, Book 6
Markus: SEALs of Honor, Book 7
Evan: SEALs of Honor, Book 8
Mason's Wish: SEALs of Honor, Book 9
Chase: SEALs of Honor, Book 10
Brett: SEALs of Honor, Book 11
Devlin: SEALs of Honor, Book 12
Easton: SEALs of Honor, Book 13
Ryder: SEALs of Honor, Book 14
Macklin: SEALs of Honor, Book 15
Corey: SEALs of Honor, Book 16
Warrick: SEALs of Honor, Book 17
Tanner: SEALs of Honor, Book 18
Jackson: SEALs of Honor, Book 19
Kanen: SEALs of Honor, Book 20
Nelson: SEALs of Honor, Book 21
SEALs of Honor, Books 1–3
SEALs of Honor, Books 4–6
SEALs of Honor, Books 7–10
SEALs of Honor, Books 11–13
SEALs of Honor, Books 14–16
SEALs of Honor, Books 17–19

Heroes for Hire

Levi's Legend: Heroes for Hire, Book 1

Stone's Surrender: Heroes for Hire, Book 2

Merk's Mistake: Heroes for Hire, Book 3

Rhodes's Reward: Heroes for Hire, Book 4

Flynn's Firecracker: Heroes for Hire, Book 5

Logan's Light: Heroes for Hire, Book 6

Harrison's Heart: Heroes for Hire, Book 7

Saul's Sweetheart: Heroes for Hire, Book 8

Dakota's Delight: Heroes for Hire, Book 9

Michael's Mercy (Part of Sleeper SEAL Series)

Tyson's Treasure: Heroes for Hire, Book 10

Jace's Jewel: Heroes for Hire, Book 11

Rory's Rose: Heroes for Hire, Book 12

Brandon's Bliss: Heroes for Hire, Book 13

Liam's Lily: Heroes for Hire, Book 14

North's Nikki: Heroes for Hire, Book 15

Anders's Angel: Heroes for Hire, Book 16

Reyes's Raina: Heroes for Hire, Book 17

Dezi's Diamond: Heroes for Hire, Book 18

Vince's Vixen: Heroes for Hire, Book 19

Heroes for Hire, Books 1–3

Heroes for Hire, Books 4–6

Heroes for Hire, Books 7–9

Heroes for Hire, Books 10–12

Heroes for Hire, Books 13–15

SEALs of Steel

Badger: SEALs of Steel, Book 1

Erick: SEALs of Steel, Book 2

Cade: SEALs of Steel, Book 3

Talon: SEALs of Steel, Book 4

Laszlo: SEALs of Steel, Book 5
Geir: SEALs of Steel, Book 6
Jager: SEALs of Steel, Book 7
The Final Reveal: SEALs of Steel, Book 8
SEALs of Steel, Books 1–4
SEALs of Steel, Books 5–8
SEALs of Steel, Books 1–8

Collections
Dare to Be You...
Dare to Love...
Dare to be Strong...
RomanceX3

Standalone Novellas
It's a Dog's Life
Riana's Revenge
Second Chances

Published Young Adult Books:

Family Blood Ties Series
Vampire in Denial
Vampire in Distress
Vampire in Design
Vampire in Deceit
Vampire in Defiance
Vampire in Conflict
Vampire in Chaos
Vampire in Crisis
Vampire in Control
Vampire in Charge

Family Blood Ties Set 1–3
Family Blood Ties Set 1–5
Family Blood Ties Set 4–6
Family Blood Ties Set 7–9
Sian's Solution, A Family Blood Ties Series Prequel
Novelette

Design series
Dangerous Designs
Deadly Designs
Darkest Designs
Design Series Trilogy

Standalone
In Cassie's Corner
Gem Stone (a Gemma Stone Mystery)
Time Thieves

Published Non-Fiction Books:

Career Essentials
Career Essentials: The Résumé
Career Essentials: The Cover Letter
Career Essentials: The Interview
Career Essentials: 3 in 1

Printed in Poland
by Amazon Fulfillment
Poland Sp. z o.o., Wrocław

57583442R00123